How I Became a Spy

Also by Deborah Hopkinson

The Great Trouble:
A Mystery of London, the Blue Death, and a Boy Called Eel

A Bandit's Tale:
The Muddled Misadventures of a Pickpocket

Into the Firestorm:
A Novel of San Francisco, 1906

HOW
I BECAME
A SPY

A Mystery of
WWII London

DEBORAH HOPKINSON

Alfred A. Knopf  New York

Text copyright © 2019 by Deborah Hopkinson
Jacket photos: skyline copyright © 2019 by Getty Images; boy copyright © 2019 by Trevillion Images; other images used under license from Shutterstock.com
Map copyright © 2019 by Robert Lazzaretti

All rights reserved. Published in the United States by Alfred A. Knopf, an imprint of Random House Children's Books, a division of Penguin Random House LLC, New York.

Knopf, Borzoi Books, and the colophon are registered trademarks of Penguin Random House LLC.

Visit us on the Web! rhcbooks.com

Educators and librarians, for a variety of teaching tools, visit us at RHTeachersLibrarians.com

Library of Congress Cataloging-in-Publication Data is available upon request.

ISBN 978-0-399-55706-4 (trade) — ISBN 978-0-399-55707-1 (lib. bdg.) — ISBN 978-0-399-55708-8 (ebook)

The text of this book is set in 12-point Galliard.

Printed in the United States of America
February 2019
10 9 8 7 6 5 4 3 2 1
First Edition

Random House Children's Books
supports the First Amendment and celebrates the right to read.

For Elisa, Barry, and especially for Katie,
who loves the real Rue, Beatrix, and Brooklyn (Hero)
just like we do

CONTENTS

64 Baker Street
Inter-Services Research Bureau (SOE)

Hanover Square

84 Charing Cross Road
Marks and Co Bookstore

Mill Street
St. George's Rectory

25 Broadwick Street
Trenchard House (Bertie's Home)

Grosvenor Square

Hay's Mews
Eleanor's House

Nelson's Column

LONDON
1944

1000   2000
feet

FRIDAY, FEBRUARY 18, 1944, DUSK
LONDON

I wasn't thinking about becoming a spy that night. I was just trying to be brave, do a good job, and stay out of trouble. It wasn't going well.

"Hold on, LR!" I pumped hard. The air-raid warning sirens hit a high, eerie crescendo, then dipped low, sending shivers down my spine. The sound made Little Roo crazy, like a giant wolf was daring her to join the pack. She threw her small black muzzle to the flare-spattered sky and howled along, her long spaniel ears flapping like flags.

My heart pounded. And it wasn't just from riding fast. Tonight was a test. I wanted to prove they hadn't made a mistake in taking me on. I wanted to do something right for once. But I wasn't following the rules for being an air-raid messenger. And (though I didn't know it yet) I *definitely* wasn't following the rules for being a spy.

Now, of course, I'm an expert.

Rule number one: Always try to blend in.

When the sirens had started up, I couldn't find my steel civil defense helmet with the *M* for *Messenger* emblazoned on the front. So I'd grabbed an old tin pan and jammed it on my flyaway red hair.

Rule number two: Don't carry any conspicuous items.

My bicycle basket should've contained my torch (what Americans call a flashlight). I'd run out without that too. Instead, it held Little Roo, otherwise known as LR. Conspicuous? She was the cutest dog in London.

Rule number three: Be alert at all times.

And maybe if I'd been paying more attention that night, I wouldn't have run into the mysterious American girl.

Then again, if that hadn't happened, I might never have become a spy.

PART ONE

The Mysterious American Girl

The agent, unlike the soldier,
who has many friends, is surrounded
by enemies, seen and unseen.

—*Special Operations Executive (SOE) Manual:*
How to Be an Agent in Occupied Europe

CHAPTER ONE

You see, but you do not observe.
—Sherlock Holmes,
in "A Scandal in Bohemia"

I kept my head down as I went around the curve, hoping the pan wouldn't fly off my head. With my right hand, I steadied my quivering spaniel and tried to keep her from toppling out of the basket. Still, even one-handed, I swear I would've made the turn with no problem.

Except. Except the girl was standing in the middle of Maddox Street. I shouted, "Hey, watch out!"

Too late. I had to let go of Little Roo. I grabbed both handlebars and pulled hard to the left. I wasn't quick enough. My right pedal struck the girl's shin; we all went down. I banged my left knee. The pan clattered away and LR tumbled out of the basket. She bounced up and began barking and twirling in circles like a crazy windup toy. Overhead, bombers roared. From the ground, ack-ack guns shot defensive fire into the sky. I scrambled to my feet, rubbing my knee.

"Are you all right?" I yelled over the din.

The girl didn't answer at first. I reached out a hand to help her up. She pushed it away. "Why don't you watch where you're going?"

"Me? You were standing in the street! You're lucky I wasn't a bus: You would've been crushed flat."

Then I stopped. Pointless. It was pointless to argue. I could tell from her accent that the girl was an American. The city was crawling with them. Soldiers in uniform, journalists, navy and army officers sporting stripes and medals, young women in crisp American Red Cross uniforms. Everyone had come to prepare for the invasion of France. It was the only way the Allies could defeat Hitler and end the war.

I knew as well as anyone that we needed the Americans, but there was a part of me that resented these strangers. They hadn't been here during the worst of it. Three years ago, the Blitz had gone on and on. We'd lived through all-night bombing raids, incendiary bombs designed to burn London to the ground, rubble and destruction on street after street. A lot of kids had been sent to the countryside. My older brother, Will, and I had begged to stay.

The Americans hadn't lived through that. Compared to us Londoners, they seemed to burst with hope and energy. Maybe they just ate better. They had money to eat in restaurants, where (so we heard) you could still get "real" food. They hadn't spent years waiting in long queues, ration cards in hand, to buy food that didn't taste much like food.

Latecomers. Too late to change what had happened to us.

Dad, as always, looked on the bright side. "We can't achieve victory without them, Bertie," he explained. "Britain needs American troops and trucks and tanks. We need them all. Be polite when you encounter anyone from the United States."

And so I tried again. "Sorry I knocked you down, miss. I'm a civil defense volunteer. It's my job to tell you to get to the shelter immediately. It's just up the street."

The girl snorted as she stood. She brushed off her coat. "You don't look very official. You look like a kid. And was that a tin pan on your head?"

I felt my face burn. "I'm thirteen. It's just . . . this is the first time I've been on duty during a raid and I couldn't find—"

That was as far as I got. All at once, the night splintered apart. *Whoomph. Bam!*

"Get down!" I hollered. I had just enough time to grab LR and throw myself to the pavement. I curled over her warm, furry body and whispered, "It'll be all right, girl."

We were lucky. I felt the ground shake, but the bomb had hit nearby, most likely a block or two away. I glanced up to check on the stranger. *What is she even doing out alone at dusk?* I wondered. Most people headed inside

7

on a late winter afternoon, especially now that the German bombing raids had begun again.

"Please, miss . . . it's not safe to be out."

The girl shot to her feet. "I've got to go."

And then she was gone, flying off down the street, her dark blue coat flapping against her thin legs. *Good,* I thought. *Maybe the noise has scared her. Maybe she'll follow directions and get to safety.*

"Go past the big church on your left," I bellowed. "You'll see the sign for the shelter to your right." I couldn't be entirely sure, but it looked as if she'd darted right past it. I shrugged. Well, she wasn't my problem. Time to get to the command post.

LR wriggled out of my arms and started sniffing around. I went searching for the tin pan to stick back on my head. Next thing I knew, LR was at my feet, tail spinning like a propeller. *Woof!* Out came a muffled bark. Her little jaws were clamped onto something. "What have you got, LR? Drop it!"

I was about to reach for the object when the sound of footsteps startled me. I turned to see an older couple passing by, heading in the same direction as the girl. "Let's go, dear," the man called to the woman. "Almost there."

"I'm a civil defense volunteer," I hollered. "Take shelter now!"

"Thanks, lad, but we're almost home," the man said, reaching out to grab his wife's hand. "We've got a Morrison shelter under our kitchen table. We'll be safe."

A hatless young man with short dark hair came bounding right behind them. I tried my warning again. "Get to the shelter!"

He shot me a frown. I had a quick impression of an angular face and intense, blazing eyes. He looked preoccupied, as if he had something else on his mind besides ack-ack guns. And then, like the other three, he hurried off down Maddox Street.

"I give up! No one pays me any attention," I complained to LR, who was still wagging and waiting for me to claim what she'd discovered. I picked up a battered red notebook, small enough to fit in my trouser pocket. I slipped it in without thinking much about it, then reached out for LR.

"Now we *really* have to go. Back in the basket!" The wardens would be disappointed in me. Disappointing people was all I seemed to be able to do.

But LR wasn't listening either. Nose to the ground, she raced past me, going back the way we'd come. She wasn't going home, was she? "Oh, come on, LR! Get back here," I snapped. "You're going to make me lose my messenger job."

I lunged. I missed. And LR kept going. She had a determined trot. And she was stubborn. If she wanted to listen, she listened. And if she didn't . . .

About all I could do was chase after her short, stubby tail with its curlicue waving at the tip. It soon became clear she wasn't heading home. She disappeared around the curve and into a small side street on the right.

LR was trained to find people in the rubble. This street hadn't been hit, though. The blast I'd just felt had been farther away. So what *was* she doing? I stopped short at the entrance to the narrow alleyway. "Little Roo!"

She'd vanished into the gloom. The sky had grown darker and the night quieter. The sirens had stopped for now; the bombers had moved on, at least from this part of the city.

I'd forgotten gloves and my hands were cold. But as I stood alone in that eerie place, my palms started to feel clammy. There was an odd prickling at the base of my neck, almost as if someone was watching me. I peered over my shoulder and squinted. I couldn't see anyone. I tried to keep breathing. In, out. In, out. It helped me stay calm. Sometimes.

If only I had my torch. Mum used to remind me about things like that. But that was before.

And then I made myself do it. I took a step into the darkness.

CHAPTER TWO

Never trust to general impressions, my boy,
but concentrate yourself upon details.

> —Sherlock Holmes, in "A Case of Identity"

"LR?" I whispered, shuffling ahead a few paces. Silence. On either side, old brick buildings hemmed me in.

I noticed some "Food Waste for Pigs" bins on my left. Was LR just nosing around for crumbs? I called again. "Little Roo?"

At last I heard a faint answering whine. As my eyes adjusted to the gloom, I spotted her. She was nosing a bulky, dark shape, past the food waste bins, on the left side of the street. It wasn't an unexploded bomb, an overturned bin, or a heap of clothes.

It was a person.

I took a shaky breath and inched forward. As I drew closer, I realized it was a young woman, lying on her side, eyes closed. Her head rested on one arm, almost as if she was asleep. Could she be asleep? One part of my brain knew that didn't make sense. No one falls asleep on the side of the street during an air raid.

She'd been wearing a hat, but it had fallen off. A few strands of wavy dark hair spilled across her cheek. She was young and pretty. But most of all, she was still. Very still.

I couldn't see much without my torch. It was impossible to tell if she had cuts or bruises. I didn't spot any blood. And she wasn't buried under smoldering rubble like a bomb victim. So what *was* she doing here? What had happened to her?

"Miss?" I managed to croak. "Miss, can you hear me? Are you hurt?"

Was she dead? I'd have to touch her to be sure. I reached out my hand, then drew it back. I made myself try again, laying the back of my hand on her forehead for just a second. I breathed a sigh of relief. She didn't feel cold. Not at all. She was alive.

Now what? I had no first-aid equipment—nothing. I tried to remember my training. I was supposed to keep victims warm. I was supposed to sound reassuring so people wouldn't panic. Most of all, I was supposed to get assistance immediately.

I took off my jacket and draped it over her chest and shoulders. "I'm going for help now, miss," I whispered.

Oh, come on, Bertie, I told myself. I cleared my throat. This time I tried to sound confident, as if I knew what

I was doing. "Miss, my name is Bertie Bradshaw. I'm a civil defense volunteer," I said in a firm, loud voice. I placed my hand on her arm in a way that I hoped was reassuring, how I imagined Warden Ita might do it. "I'll return as soon as I can. Please remain calm."

It sounded ridiculous even to my own ears. I got to my feet, swept up LR in my arms, and ran. I felt guilty leaving her there.

Yet, even at that moment, I had a strange feeling. Even then, I felt a prickling in my mind. I had missed something—some tiny, significant detail.

I rushed back to my bicycle, plunked LR in the basket, and pedaled hard. I hadn't gone far when the all clear sounded with its steady, high note. A short raid! Good. Especially since I'd forgotten to stick the pan back on my head.

A few minutes later, I stumbled through the doorway of the civil defense command post, LR bouncing along at my heels. Like the public shelter nearby, it was a reinforced building. It had been built after the Blitz.

As far as the civil defense was concerned, when a bomb struck, that was an "incident." I thought it was a funny word to have chosen. It felt dry and cold. It didn't capture what really happened: People died; families lost their homes or their shops. London was full of the remnants of past *incidents*. You could still see piles of rubble, like great, gaping scars. You couldn't always see the scars on people.

Little Roo stopped to lap water from a bowl in the corner, making a noisy mess. No one would mind. She was the post's mascot. In the back office, the two senior wardens studied a large map of London that covered almost the entire wall, with an insert for our section. They marked active fires and bombing incidents on a chalkboard.

On the desk sat a phone, though it wasn't always reliable during air raids since the phone lines often went down. That's why we messengers were needed. And that's why I was in trouble.

"Get to the command post as soon as you can," they'd said during training. "Messengers carry critical information to rescue and fire crews and ambulance stations. Your work is dangerous, but it helps save lives."

I'd been too young to volunteer during the Blitz, three years ago. And I guess technically I should've been fourteen. But after I turned thirteen in August, I'd begged Dad to put in a good word for me, and I got in. I think he agreed to let me join only because no one had expected the attacks to start up again. But then, a few weeks into the new year, there'd been a raid. Then another. And now, tonight, another. Hitler hadn't forgotten about us. Would 1944 turn out to be as bad as 1940 and 1941?

"Um—um, excuse me," I stammered. I wondered if

they'd send me home and tell me not to come back. Messengers weren't supposed to report for duty *after* the all-clear siren.

"Well, look who finally decided to show his face." The short older man, Warden Hawksworth, turned his keen gaze on me. Everyone called him Warden Hawk, and it wasn't just because of his name. The wizened old police officer had sharp blue eyes and a beaklike nose.

"What's wrong, Bertie?" Warden Ita stepped toward me. "Did you come across incendiary bombs? Do we need to call in a fire crew?"

Warden Ita was tall and handsome, with a warm smile, soft brown eyes, and glowing dark skin. Even though the two wardens looked so different on the outside, I always thought of them as being alike. They were so dedicated to their work and to the people of London. They helped us believe we'd all get through this together.

On the first day of our messenger training, Warden Hawk had welcomed us to the civil defense. "You're leaders now, and the community will look up to you. When you pin on that civil defense badge, you pledge yourself to be diligent and fearless."

"Now, we don't expect messengers to perform heroic deeds, of course. We just ask that you do your best. And remember, each of us is brave in our own way," Warden Ita had added, in his deep, elegant voice. "Sometimes being brave is just taking one step at a time."

I'd almost run out of the room at that point. Someone

like me didn't belong in the civil defense. I wasn't courageous. I most definitely wasn't a hero. And because of
that, bad things had happened to my family. My brother
had almost died because of me.

"Bertie?" Warden Ita asked again.

"No, sir. It's not a fire," I said. "I found . . . that is,
Little Roo found a woman."

"Do you know the address—or at least the street?"
Warden Hawk barked, grabbing a pin to mark the incident location on his map.

"Um . . . I'm not really sure, sir." Street signs had
been removed early in the war, to confuse the Germans
if they did invade. "It's a small street off Maddox, right
before a bend. It's just before the big old stone church
with the columns—"

"St. George's, Hanover Square," they finished for me.

Warden Ita glanced at the map for a second. "Yes. I
think you must've been on Mill Street, Bertie."

Warden Hawk nodded his agreement. Like Dad, the
wardens knew almost every street in London. Warden
Hawk had walked them for years as a police officer. And
since arriving in England from Nigeria, Warden Ita had
worked part-time as a postman.

"That's strange, though. We received a call about an
incident closer to Hanover Square," said Warden Hawk,
walking over to join Warden Ita at the map. "But we
don't have any reports of damage on Mill Street."

"No, sir. I should have said that first," I told them.

"She isn't . . . that is, I don't think she's a bomb victim. She's not trapped in rubble. The woman's not *inside* at all. She's just lying *on* the pavement, on the side of the street. Huddled against a building, really. And I didn't . . . I didn't see any blood."

"Is she dead, Bertie?" Warden Ita asked gently.

"No, sir." I shook my head. "But her eyes were closed and she didn't respond to my questions. I did remember to tell her to keep calm, sir."

Warden Ita raised his eyebrows and I saw his lips twitch. "Good work, Bertie. I'll call the police station and the ambulance service and ask them to send someone over. Luckily, the phone lines weren't hit tonight."

He was already moving toward the desk. "Funny, I can't recall any young woman living on Mill Street. Mostly shops and offices there. She might be just a passing pedestrian who fainted."

"Come on, then. I'll pedal back with you, Bertie." Warden Hawk pulled his coat off a hook. Reaching into a pocket, he slipped LR a biscuit.

Warden Hawk might be crusty, but he had a soft spot for LR. Sometimes I wondered if he wished he had taken her in himself when her owners moved away. "They want her to keep on as a rescue dog," Warden Hawk had said when he'd brought her to our flat in the fall. "They asked me to find a happy home for her."

Warden Hawk had glanced at Dad. "Now that Bertie has finished his civil defense training, I thought he might be just the one to care for her. The lady who owned her was a children's librarian. That's how she got her name, from Roo in *Winnie-the-Pooh*. Anyway, she's about three now, so they've asked that her name not be changed."

Little Roo had snuggled into my arms like she belonged there. Her eyes were wide and brown and trusting. She'd tucked her warm, wet muzzle under my chin and heaved a little sigh.

Warden Hawk had known me since I was a baby. He'd been Dad's mentor in the police force. He was good at asking questions and prying out information. And as we hurried out of the command post, I found myself dreading the bicycle ride ahead—and the interrogation I'd probably face.

Warden Hawk might have brought LR to us. But he definitely knew our home was not a happy one.

CHAPTER THREE

[The agent] should not only observe things but also make deductions from them.

—*SOE Manual*

Happy. Little Roo was far from it. She'd had enough of riding in the bike basket for one night.

"Stay put, LR," I snapped. I was anxious and restless too. What if I'd been gone too long? Would the woman still be alive?

I stole a glance at Warden Hawk, riding beside me on a bicycle not much bigger than mine. If I didn't want to be questioned about how things were going at home, I'd have to steer the conversation to something else. And I knew just how to distract him. You could *always* get Warden Hawk to talk about military strategy.

"Uh, Warden," I began, "do you . . . do you think these new bombing raids will turn out to be as bad as the Blitz?"

"I don't think so, Bertie. More like a little Blitz, if

you ask me," he replied, reaching up one hand to adjust his tin helmet. "Hitler's just trying to get revenge. But he's running out of planes."

"Why's that?"

"Allied pilots have been hitting German cities hard for months now. We've put the German air force on the defensive, no doubt about it. As I understand it, we're hoping to weaken the Luftwaffe before the invasion. We don't want those German bombers buzzing overhead when our boys land in France."

"Do you think the invasion will be soon, sir?"

"Ah, well, I read in the *Times* that Dwight D. Eisenhower has arrived to take charge as supreme commander of the Allied Expeditionary Force. Quite a mouthful, ain't it? Though if you want my opinion, nothing will happen till spring," Warden Hawk went on. "That should give him time enough to put the finishing touches on the operation."

I smiled a little. My plan to distract him was working. Warden Hawk reminded me of our history teacher, Mr. Turner, an elderly gentleman who'd returned to teaching when our regular instructor had joined the Royal Navy. All you had to do was ask Mr. Turner one question about the war, and he'd be off like a runaway horse.

"The invasion has to wait until spring or early summer. It's just common sense if you think about it: The English Channel is simply too rough in winter," Warden

Hawk was saying. "If you tried to ferry thousands of troops across to France in high seas, why, they'd be too seasick to fight when they hit the beaches. No, you need calm seas and fair weather."

"But won't the Germans know it too?" I wondered. "Won't they be waiting for the Allied troops?"

"Oh, they know an assault is coming; make no mistake about that," Warden Hawk replied. "Hitler's built his Atlantic Wall of defenses up and down the coast of France and then some. But here's the thing: The Nazis don't know precisely when or where we will invade. And I'll tell you something else, Bertie. I sure wouldn't want to be in charge of keeping *that* information secret."

When we reached Mill Street, we parked our bicycles. I'd been hoping Warden Hawk's lecture on the Allied invasion might keep him from noticing I didn't have my torch. No such luck.

"It's a wonder you could see anything in that alleyway," he said. "Look at you: No helmet. No torch. No civil defense badge or whistle either. You have to do better next time, Bertie."

"Yes, sir. I know. I was just so excited to be on duty. . . ." My voice trailed off. Even I had to admit my excuse sounded pretty lame. At least there would be a next time.

I lifted LR out of the basket and she raced over to

where a young policeman stood on the corner. Planting her paws, she began to bark.

I tried to pull her back while Warden Hawk stepped forward to shake the man's hand. "You got here quick enough."

"Good evening, Warden Hawk," said Constable Jimmy Wilson. "Hullo there, Bertie."

"Hi, Jimmy. Stop barking, LR!" Jimmy was new to the police force, but he was already one of my favorites. "Sorry. She's all riled up tonight. I guess because it's our first raid together."

At that moment, another figure emerged from the shadows of Mill Street.

"Is she all right?" I asked.

"Is who all right?" Constable George Morton scowled as he strode over to me, hands on hips.

"The woman—" I began.

"Come on, Bertie. What are you on about?" George cut me off. "Warden Ita called us to say one of his messengers found a victim. We don't have time for wild goose chases."

My mouth flew open. Before I could say a word, George turned to Warden Hawk. "There's no one here, Warden."

"But . . . but there was! I swear there was a woman." I felt my face get hot. "I wouldn't lie about it."

George spoke in a low voice to Jimmy and Warden Hawk. I caught only bits and pieces, but it was enough to make me clench my fists. "His dad says . . . having a hard time . . ."

Jimmy shrugged. "Well, maybe Bertie did see someone. She might've just got to her feet and left."

"Wait!" I cried. I'd been pedaling so hard I hadn't been cold, but now I remembered. "I put my jacket over her. Is it there?"

George shrugged. "Don't think so. And there's no sign of any neighbors out and about. Mostly shops on this street, anyway."

"Go on and look for your jacket, Bertie." Warden Hawk handed me his torch.

I trotted off. I swept the narrow passage with my light, making eerie shadows on the old brick buildings. There were the bins. But nothing lay near them. No jacket. No young woman. No body. But she *had* been here. Could she have just walked off?

Back on Maddox Street, an ambulance had pulled up. I heard Warden Hawk tell the driver it was a false alarm. "That's all right, Warden," I heard her say through the window. "It's always nice to see you. Besides, we're headed to the morgue and it was on our way."

She stepped on the gas and the vehicle rumbled off, its hooded headlights just tiny slits. The morgue. My mind whirled with another possibility. Maybe the woman had died. Could someone have moved her body in the short time I was gone? But she hadn't been dead when I'd found her. I was sure of that.

I found myself looking at George Morton. He'd emerged alone out of the darkness. *Don't be ridiculous,* I told myself. George didn't know her. He couldn't have had anything to do with this.

But I trusted what I'd seen. Little Roo had found a young woman. I'd draped my jacket over her. And now she had disappeared, along with my coat.

There had to be an answer to this puzzle. I just had no idea what it was.

CHAPTER FOUR

The agent . . . has only his alertness,
initiative and observation to help him. He
has to look after himself but we can prepare
him for this by training.

                                    —SOE Manual

"Hullo, Bertie, you're back late." The young constable at the reception desk at Trenchard House called out a greeting. "Did the little dog rescue anyone?"

"No, we were lucky tonight. No rescues needed." I waved good night and pushed my bicycle along the hallway, LR trotting behind.

Our flat was on the main floor, close to the reception desk, since Dad was the building caretaker as well as a police sergeant. When I'd first told friends at school that I lived in a boardinghouse with more than a hundred policemen, they'd made stupid jokes about it. "You better be careful, Bertie, or you'll get hauled off to jail for not doing your homework." Or "I'm not coming to your house, Bertie. I don't want to get put in prison."

David was the only friend who'd ever visited me here.

It wasn't just that he lived close by, on Berwick Street. David dreamed of being a detective one day. He liked to hang about Trenchard House, hoping to pick up some tips.

"These aren't real detective inspectors," I told him. "They're just young constables who complain about how their feet hurt from walking all over the city."

"You can never tell what you might learn from just listening," David replied. "As the great detective himself said, 'You know my method. It is founded upon the observation of trifles.' That's from 'The Boscombe Valley Mystery.' "

I'd never be a Sherlock Holmes expert like David. Or like my brother, Will.

Trenchard House wasn't a good place to learn to be a detective. And it wasn't much of a home either. We'd moved here only after we lost our own house. I knew not to complain. "No one in London can count on having a roof overhead from one day to the next," Dad said. "We're lucky we found a place to stay, unlike some of our neighbors."

Our flat had two small bedrooms off the kitchen, and a tiny parlor where Dad sat in a bulky old armchair to read the newspaper. We didn't even have room for an indoor Morrison shelter. Some people put these cagelike metal structures under dining tables, but our table sat only four. It didn't matter much. Since so many people lived in Trenchard House, we had a designated underground shelter in Soho Square.

At our old house, Dad had installed an Anderson shelter in the back garden. He'd had to dig down four feet and cover the corrugated metal roof with soil. We all fit fine. It was six feet tall, about that same length, and four and a half feet wide. I remembered, because Will and I had helped Dad measure out the space. Anderson shelters were good protection, unless there was a direct hit.

But, of course, you had to get there in time. I tried not to think about our old Anderson shelter. And how we weren't in it on the one night that mattered.

LR shot through the door of the flat and curled up on her bed in the kitchen. It still surprised me—how quiet and empty it always seemed. Before, Mum would have had the kettle whistling. "Tea and toast. That's what you need," she always said.

Mum had always had tea and toast and homemade berry jam ready after school, or when Dad returned from patrol with red, chafed cheeks and tiny icicles on the ends of his long mustache. Now I made my own tea and toast, though we'd finished the last of the jam. Sometimes the toast came out burnt and hard. Not even Little Roo would eat that. When we first got her, I'd worried about having enough to feed her. But she gobbled most anything. Once, she seized an egg that fell and broke. LR chewed it up, shell and all, before I could pry it out of her mouth. I almost laughed, but since we each got only one *real* egg every week, it wasn't that funny.

I felt hungry, but too tired to bother. It would be easier just to go to bed. I didn't want to sit alone with my thoughts—the American girl, the missing woman in the alley, our empty flat. I didn't want to think about how lonely it was without Mum and Will.

Dad had left a note on the kitchen table saying he'd be late. These days he spent most of his time on duty making sure people weren't looting. If anything big happened, he had to call the real detectives from Scotland Yard to take charge.

I didn't need to ask Scotland Yard what was wrong in our family. That's another thing the war had taught me. Some things can't be fixed by tea and toast.

SATURDAY

I woke early. LR had moved from the foot of the bed to stick her wet nose in my face. "It's Saturday," I cried. "Let me sleep a little longer."

But as I lay there, everything from the night before came rushing back. The missing woman. The American girl. The notebook. The notebook! I reached to the floor and pulled it out of my trousers.

I looked for the owner's name but couldn't see one anywhere. Most likely, the American girl had dropped it. Maybe I shouldn't have started to scan the pages, but I was curious.

I switched on my bedside lamp and lay back against my pillow. LR rested her chin on my knee, fixing her round eyes on me. "We'll go out in a minute," I promised. "Maybe this is her diary or her school notes."

I suppose it's weird to talk to your dog like she can understand everything. Sometimes LR cocked her head as if she was concentrating hard on what I said. Probably she was only waiting to hear her favorite words: *walk*, and *go*, and *treat*.

And then I began to read. The first sentence jumped out at me.

The invasion is coming. That's the key. The key to everything I'll learn here, and why I'm training for this dangerous mission.

No one can say when the invasion will happen, or exactly where the troops will land. But now I have a part to play. I can do something to help win this awful war.

CHAPTER FIVE

If you follow conscientiously in the field
all that we teach you here, we cannot
guarantee your safety, but we think that your
chance of being picked up is very small.
Remember that the best agents are never
caught.

—SOE Manual

My mouth fell open. I shot up so fast, LR toppled onto
the bedclothes. What in the world? What was this notebook, anyway? I took a breath and kept reading.

Today was our first lecture. We have a field instructor, a
code master, and someone who seems to be the boss in
charge of all operations. We'll start in the classroom but
later I'll learn about explosives and wireless radios.

Our instructor explained that there will be two phases
to our work: pre-invasion and post-invasion. When we are
sent into the field—into our assigned countries—we must
help prepare for the day when soldiers will liberate the
people from German occupation.

He also explained that our organization is relatively
new, and was formed at the beginning of the war. It's

called the SOE, the Special Operations Executive, and it's top-secret. "Sometimes SOE agents are called the Baker Street Irregulars, like the ragtag bunch of urchins Sherlock Holmes relied on to gather information. And, of course, our headquarters are there, though you wouldn't know it from the sign on the building." He gave a sly smile.

Secrecy is essential. I was supposed to hand over all writing materials. (I honestly forgot I had this small notebook tucked away in my suitcase.) So I'm already breaking the rules. But then, I always do. When Maman died, I left home to strike out on my own. I haven't done what other girls do. And now I've done <u>this</u>.

I know I must be careful. No one must ever find this notebook.

Those words stopped me cold. No one must ever find this notebook.

But I had found it. Who did it really belong to? I remembered what David had told me. To solve his cases, Sherlock Holmes had depended on "the observation of trifles." I should use that same method now.

I considered the notebook in my hand. It was battered and well used, but not damp or crushed. It couldn't have been lying in the street for more than a few minutes. Otherwise, it would've been run over by a vehicle or trod upon. Or it would be soggy from cold, wet fog.

"LR, my observations lead me to the conclusion that the American girl dropped it," I told my furry Watson, who'd gone back to sleep and was snoring gently. "But here's the important question: Is she the person who wrote in it?"

Hold on a minute! I snapped my fingers. Little Roo had run to Mill Street. Could my spaniel have picked up the scent of the young woman in the alley from this notebook? And if the notebook did belong to her, then why did the American girl have it?

My head felt like it would burst with questions. Maybe I could find clues to the owner's identity in the notebook. I started reading again.

But even though it may be wrong, I'm going to keep taking notes. Besides, I don't want to fail this training course. And I know I won't remember anything if I don't write some things down. I'll begin with the first three rules for being a secret agent:

> Always try to blend in.
> Don't carry any conspicuous items.
> Be alert at all times.

Tomorrow we learn about surveillance (how to follow someone secretly) and what to do if we're being followed once we're living undercover in a country occupied by the Nazis. I'm excited and a bit frightened too. But I'm determined to see this through.

By now, I couldn't stop reading. I could feel my pulse quicken as I turned one page, then the next. I scanned sections, amazed at what I found. Words kept jumping out at me: Nazi occupation, surveillance, cover story, sabotage, concealment, enemy forces, resistance, espionage. Parachute.

Parachute! So that must be how secret agents entered countries occupied by the Nazis. The thought of it made me shiver. I'd always wanted to ride in a plane, but I couldn't imagine jumping out of one.

About halfway through the notebook, the neat penmanship abruptly stopped. Instead, the pages were filled with cramped, hasty scribbles, almost as if the writer was scribbling in the dark or riding in a moving vehicle. I didn't stop to read, but kept turning the pages.

Then I stared. And frowned. "Hold on a minute. What's this?"

I stumbled out of bed and went to the window. LR hopped down and followed me, tail wiggling hopefully. "We'll go in a minute, LR. Let me look at this. Because I don't understand what I'm seeing here."

I raised the blackout blinds to let in more light. That didn't help. There was page after page of writing. The writing wasn't in another language like Latin, which I'd studied a little in school (though I hadn't done very well). And it didn't use a different alphabet, like Chinese or Russian. It was the English alphabet, all right. But the letters weren't in any order that made sense.

They weren't even arranged into words with spaces in between. A lot of this notebook was simply a series of random letters.

Gibberish. Unreadable. This was some sort of secret writing system.

This notebook *couldn't* just be some made-up story the American girl was writing for fun. I felt almost certain it belonged to an actual secret agent—someone in the resistance.

Mr. Turner, our history teacher, spoke often of the resistance. He listened to the BBC Radio news broadcast every night at nine and read the *Times* every morning. Whenever we walked into our classroom, we'd find him moving pins to track Allied battle positions on a large wall map. The map also showed the countries the Nazis occupied, including France and Denmark.

"In October of 1943, the Nazis planned raids to round up all the Jews in Denmark," Mr. Turner had told us. "Thanks to an early warning, ordinary Danes helped seven thousand of their Jewish neighbors escape to Sweden.

"And, of course, before the war began, people here in Great Britain played a part in helping ten thousand Jewish children escape the Nazis. As you know, we've welcomed a few Jewish refugees at this school."

At that, I'd glanced over at David. He was staring down at his old wooden desk, tracing circles with his finger. David hadn't heard from his parents in more than two years. When we'd first become friends, I'd some-times ask him if he'd gotten a letter.

Then one day he'd said, "Don't ask me about letters anymore, Bertie."

Now I slammed the red notebook shut. I looked around my room for a hiding place: two narrow beds, a small bookcase, my bicycle in the corner. In the end, I slipped it under Will's mattress.

I finished dressing and tiptoed across the kitchen floor. I knew Dad would want to sleep in after his late shift. I grabbed LR's lead.

David attended morning service at his synagogue, but I had to talk to him for just a few minutes. David's foster father and mother ran a shoe shop at the edge of the Berwick Street Market. The family lived on the second floor. So when the shop was closed, it was easier to toss a pebble at David's window than knock on a door.

I did that now, and David threw up the window and stuck his head out. "Hey, Bertie. What's up?"

"Hi. Um, well. I just wanted to ask you. How much do you know about ciphers?"

David grinned. "I know a little, mostly from reading Sherlock Holmes. He cracked a cipher in a story called 'The Adventure of the Dancing Men.'" He leaned his elbows on the sill and lowered his voice. "Hey, so why do you want to know? Did you overhear something at Trenchard House? Did you find a case we can work on?"

I shook my head. "No, nothing like that." I hesitated. I didn't think it was a good idea to start talking about secret agents in the middle of the street. "I'd just like to know more about them."

David wasn't buying my sudden interest in ciphers. "You can't fool me, Bertie. I bet you've stumbled on some unsolved case, a real mystery. Tomorrow I have to help in the shop, but I'll bring the story to school on Monday so you can borrow it. Wait till you read it!"

I waved goodbye and started toward home, thinking about my next steps. If the notebook was real, I should probably turn it over to the wardens at the command post—or even to Dad. I should probably never look at it again.

But that wasn't what I was about to do.

"Let's go have some breakfast, LR," I said. "Then we'll try to find that mysterious American girl."

Spy Practice Number One

SUBSTITUTION CIPHER

A substitution cipher is a cipher in which each letter of the regular alphabet is substituted for a different character. In some types, the cipher alphabet is shifted. In others, it might be completely jumbled or based on a key word or phrase. In this first example, the cipher alphabet replaces *A* with the first letter of the answer in the hint, and then the letters continue in order. For instance, if the answer to the hint began with the letter *S*, that's how you would begin your cipher alphabet. Every *A* would be an *S*; *B* would be *T*; and *C* would become *U*. It's helpful to write out the regular alphabet with the cipher alphabet underneath it. No spaces have been left between words.

qngwcizmjmqvoeibkpmlqbqamaamvb
qitnwzgwcbwjmieizmwnqb

Hint: In this message, the first letter of the cipher alphabet is the same as the first letter of the nickname of the supreme commander of the Allied Expeditionary Force, who arrived in London in January 1944 to lead the invasion of France and the efforts to defeat Nazi Germany in Europe.

You can find the supreme commander's nickname by researching his name in another book or on the internet. You can also find his name and nickname later in this story, and in the resources in the back of this book.

By the way, you don't have to decode this message to understand the story. But if you're thinking of becoming a spy someday, the practice can't hurt. (And yes, the answer is in the back.)

CHAPTER SIX

I may be on the trail in this matter, or I
may be following a will-o'-the-wisp, but I
shall soon know which it is.

—Sherlock Holmes,
in "The Adventure of the Beryl Coronet"

When Will was three years old, our grandfather gave him his first collection of Sherlock Holmes stories. My first memories are of lying in the dark, with Will telling me the adventures of the great detective.

Maybe that's one reason I liked David so much. He reminded me of Will. And maybe David could help me learn to be a detective. As for becoming a spy, well, I knew nothing—except what I'd read in the small red notebook.

"I don't think we need to confront the American girl right away," I told LR. "We'll just follow her around, secret like. Of course, we have to find her first."

I turned onto Broadwick Street. From Dad, I knew it used to be called Broad Street. It was famous for being part of a different kind of detective story. "There was a terrible cholera epidemic here in 1854," Dad had told me. "At the time, everyone thought cholera was caused by bad air. Everyone except a man named Dr. John Snow. He believed people were getting sick from using water from a well right up the block from where Trenchard House stands today. Even though he didn't have a microscope able to see cholera bacteria in the water, Dr. Snow gathered evidence to prove that contaminated well water was the real culprit."

Dad loved telling stories about London history. Just last week, when I'd asked if he ever got tired of patrolling, he'd pulled on a corner of his mustache to think about it. Then he'd said, "No, I don't. Because when I walk around London, it's almost as if I can touch the spirits of everyone who lived here in the past. And that's another reason we can't let Hitler destroy London."

At Trenchard House, LR pulled me down the hall. Sure enough, Dad was having breakfast. He'd made powdered eggs, which I could barely swallow. They were so disgusting. He'd cooked sausages too, which tasted like cardboard. I was afraid to ask what was in them.

"Ah, there you are, Bertie. I've made you a plate." The toast was burnt and the tea lukewarm. Dad wasn't much of a cook. That had been Mum's department.

Dad eyed me over his teacup. His cheeks looked hollow and shadowed. "I came home from my shift while you were out last night. I happened to see your civil defense helmet sticking up from under the dog's blanket in the corner here." He cleared his throat. "Being an air-raid messenger is serious business, Bertie. It can be dangerous and I only agreed to let you—"

"I know, Dad. I know! And I'm sorry. The siren went off and I was so excited because it was our first raid. I couldn't find my helmet and I didn't want to be late," I babbled. Before Dad could open his mouth to reply, I added, "I did grab a pan and stick it on my head."

I scraped the blackest parts from my toast. LR gave a little whine and wiggled her backside in anticipation. I tossed her half of the piece and she stood on her two hind legs to catch it in one gulp.

Dad was not about to be distracted by LR's cuteness. "I bet Warden Hawk was none too pleased to see you show up without your regulation helmet. Did it go all right, then?"

"There was an incident near Hanover Square. But the wardens said no one was hurt."

"Anything else happen?" Dad wiped one corner of his mustache with a napkin.

He knows, I thought. He must have already talked to the two young constables. "Uh, well, we found a woman lying on the street. Jimmy Wilson and George Morton were on duty. But by the time they arrived, she was gone. Maybe she'd just fainted for a few minutes." I paused for a minute, wondering if George had complained about me. "I really did see her."

Dad kept chewing. I could make out dark circles under his eyes. He looked thin and miserable. Maybe it was because of all the extra shifts he took on. The police force was short of men, due to the war. On top of that, he was responsible for just about everything at Trenchard House, from plumbing to young police officers who stayed out too late at dances and couldn't get up for their shifts the next day.

Sometimes, though, I wondered if he volunteered to work more than was necessary. When we did eat together, we mostly sat silently, looking down at our beans on toast or awful boiled cabbage.

"I'm taking the train to Surrey to visit Mum and Will this afternoon," said Dad. "Why don't you come, Bertie? You haven't seen them since the holidays. Will's doing much better. I know he'd love to see you. Mum too."

"I really can't, Dad. Maybe next time," I said. "I have history homework to do for Mr. Turner. And, uh . . . also . . . an American near the shelter last night dropped her glove. I want to see if I can find her." I spat out the lie like it was a mouthful of tasteless dried eggs. "Do you know where most of the Americans stay? I thought I could maybe bring it to a lost and found or something."

Dad took a sip of his tea. He liked to take his time to answer questions. LR scuttled to his side and gazed up, her round eyes never leaving his plate. He tossed her a tiny crust. "Here you go, you little beggar. Let's see, most of the American military officials are clustered in Mayfair near the American embassy, in those office buildings around Grosvenor Square. So many, they're calling it Little America. You're bound to see lots of American jeeps lined up to ferry generals around town. The supreme commander has his headquarters there too. And you might try Claridge's, the hotel on Brook Street, for a lost and found." He paused to toss LR another bit of toast, then launched in. "Now, you know Grosvenor Square has an interesting history."

I poured myself more lukewarm tea. Once Dad got started, you just had to wait.

"John Adams, the second American president, lived at Grosvenor Square for almost three years, beginning in 1785."

I rolled my eyes. "That's interesting, Dad. But in Mr. Turner's class, we're still back in AD 43, learning about the Roman emperor Claudius invading Britain."

"Well, anyway, there have been Americans around Grosvenor Square ever since— Oh, and I think there's a plaque on the house where Adams lived."

"I'd better get going, then. I wouldn't want to miss *that*."

"There's no call to be cheeky, son," Dad said. "Just because your mum's not—"

"Sorry," I grumbled, cutting him off before he could keep scolding me. I brought my plate and cup to the sink and reached for a jacket hanging on a peg by the door.

"Where's *your* coat, Bertie?" Dad's voice had an even sharper edge now.

"I . . . I don't know." And that was true.

"Look at me, Bertie," he said sternly.

I turned, heart pounding.

"I've done my part. I let you join the civil defense, and take in the dog," he said slowly.

I started. He wouldn't threaten to get rid of LR, would he?

"Now it's up to you," Dad went on. "Do you remember what you agreed to do when I let you join the civil defense as a messenger?"

"Yes, sir," I whispered. "I need to be responsible, reliable, and . . . uh, respectful."

"That goes for the command post *and* home." Dad ran a hand through his hair. "You know this is a hard time for us. I can't buy you anything new. You'll just have to get by. And you can't wear that. I'm taking it to Surrey today so Will can wear it."

Silently, we both looked at the coat. One of the arms would have to be pinned up.

"I'm sorry, Dad," I mumbled. "I'll try harder."

I pulled my old jacket from another peg. The sleeves were so short my wrists stuck out. I'd taken off LR's lead, but now I clipped it to her collar again and moved toward the door.

"Aren't you forgetting something, Bertie?"

Forgetting something? "Oh, uh . . . the glove. Yeah,

I have it." I patted my trouser pocket and hurried out. I'd have to do better at a lot of things—including keeping my story straight.

I should've paid more attention to something else too: the notebook. I'd skimmed through pages of lecture notes. But I'd missed this part: Whenever you are going anywhere on secret work, you must automatically take routine precautions which will make it difficult for you to be secretly watched.

Routine precautions. I should've worn a cap to cover my hair, which was almost as bright red as a London bus. I should've left LR at home so I wouldn't be so conspicuous. And I definitely should have paid more attention to my surroundings.

I was thinking of myself only as a watcher. I didn't imagine that I might be secretly watched.

CHAPTER SEVEN

Do not walk or hang about in places where you
could easily be watched without detecting it.

—SOE Manual

First task: retracing my steps to Mill Street. I wanted
to see if I'd missed anything in the darkness the night
before—anything that might offer a clue about the
young woman. The missing woman who might or might
not be a secret agent.

But it just seemed like any other London side street
on a cold day. LR sniffed around the bins. "That's not
for you, girl. The sign says 'Food Waste for Pigs.'"

LR cocked her head, as if questioning why pigs out-
ranked her: *How come they get leftover food and I don't?*

I grinned and told her, "Take my word for it, Little
Roo. You definitely don't want to be a pig. For starters,
pigs don't get to sleep in soft beds." I decided not to
mention bacon and sausages.

I took one last look at the street. It all seemed

perfectly normal. *At least,* I thought, *there aren't any bloodstains I missed in the dark.*

Then I headed over to the next block, closer to Hanover Square, to look at the incident site. The bomb had missed most of the buildings, though one wall of a shop had been blasted away. I stopped to watch crews check for unexploded bombs and shovel debris off the road.

A hand landed on my shoulder. I whirled around to find Constable George Morton. "You're awful jumpy, Bertie," he said. "These new bombing raids making you nervous, are they?"

I moved away a few steps. But LR tackled George with glee, jumping up on his trouser legs, snuffling and wagging her tail. For some reason, he was one of her favorites. "You startled me is all. Where's Jimmy?"

"Jimmy? He's off today," George said shortly. "We don't always work together. And thank goodness for that."

"I thought you were friends."

George shook his head and looked away. "I don't . . . oh, never mind."

How could anyone *not* like Jimmy? But then, George wasn't the friendly sort. "His bark is worse than his bite," Dad had told me once. "I remember him as a cheery, eager constable. He loved to dance and was popular with his mates. He left the force to enlist. But after Dunkirk in 1940 . . ."

"What happened there?"

"George was on the beach, waiting to be evacuated, when his right cheek was blown away by shrapnel," Dad had explained. "He's still bitter. I just hope he doesn't let that bitterness eat him up from the inside out."

I knew George didn't go with Jimmy and the others to Saturday-night dances. Instead, he usually took an extra shift on the reception desk, where he'd sit bent over a book, his hand half hiding his scars. Now the young constable brought his face close to mine. "Want a better look? Is this close enough for you?"

"Sorry. I . . . I didn't mean to stare," I mumbled. "I just wondered: Does . . . does it still hurt?"

"Oh, leave me alone, Bertie," he spat. "Where are you off to, anyway? Going to chase your mysterious woman?"

"No. No . . . I . . . I'm heading to Grosvenor Square," I said. "Just to look around. I hear it's really busy there now, with lots of American soldiers and jeeps."

"Preparing for the invasion, I guess," George said. He looked at the wreckage before us. "About time." He turned back to me. "Everyone says it's going to be massive. All of England has filled up with soldiers and supplies. I bet there's a few of Hitler's pals that would give a pretty penny to know the details of this operation."

"But that's top-secret, isn't it?" I asked, thinking of what I'd read in the notebook.

"Sure. Though I imagine it's not easy to keep something this enormous under wraps," George said. "And don't underestimate the power of money."

"Money?" I frowned. "You mean there might be people who sell secrets for money?"

"Yes, there could be traitors or double agents right here in London," he said, lowering his voice. I noticed his eyes were shadowed too, like Dad's. The constables didn't always get much sleep. "Nothing would surprise me."

George reached down to tug gently on LR's ear. She rolled over on her back and he scratched her belly. "LR, love, you're lucky to be a dog. Take care of Messenger Boy, just in case he turns up any more bodies—dead or alive."

As we walked away, I couldn't stop mulling over George's words. Was he so bitter about what had happened to him that he would turn against his own country as a kind of revenge?

I thought back to last night. Jimmy had been waiting on the corner. George had come out of the alleyway alone. Had he been following that woman? Was he somehow after the notebook? There certainly seemed to be secrets in it.

I had to stop thinking this way. George Morton was a constable and a decorated veteran. Besides, he never would've mentioned selling secrets if he himself was doing it. *Or would he?* I shook my head. This notebook had me thinking everyone was a traitor. On the other hand, not all of this was in my imagination. The notebook was real.

. . .

My mind was still spinning when I reached Grosvenor Square, a large, open park in the Mayfair area. I felt a little out of place: Mayfair was definitely grander than Soho.

The square bustled. Men in crisp uniforms rushed in and out of buildings. Jeeps buzzed to and fro. When they stopped, their drivers hopped out, opened doors, and saluted their superiors smartly. I spotted a few women too, in tidy blue American Red Cross uniforms and caps.

"I can see why they call it Little America," I said to LR. We walked around for a while; then I found an empty bench on the north side of the park. "I see lots of military folks, but not many civilians, or families with children."

And definitely no mysterious American girl in a dark blue coat.

LR stuck out her pink tongue and plunked down across my shoes. I sat on my hands for a while to keep them warm. Everyone else seemed too busy to sit, especially when it was so gray and gloomy out. I noticed just one man on a nearby bench. He wore a black coat, and I couldn't see his face, since his head was buried in his newspaper.

"I remember this one Sherlock Holmes story Will told me about, where he says he's not sure if he's after something real or just a will-o'-the-wisp," I told LR.

"Maybe that girl was a ghostly apparition—a figment of my imagination."

No, I had evidence: the notebook. The girl was real, but it was stupid to think I could find her again right away, even though she'd headed in this direction. Maybe she lived somewhere near here. Or maybe she was a visitor, staying at a hotel. Did tourists visit London in wartime? I didn't think so. After all, everyone knew the Atlantic Ocean was full of marauding German U-boats.

I yawned. I was on duty later at the command post. I thought of what Dad had said. If I wanted to keep volunteering, I needed to be more responsible. That meant going home and doing my history homework and making sure all my civil defense gear was in order. It didn't mean traipsing around London like I was in a spy story.

"Let's go, LR." From the north end of Grosvenor Square, we headed east along Brook Street, past Claridge's.

A glimpse inside the hotel revealed a sparkling entryway and guests in fancy clothes. In case Dad asked me, I'd say I'd dropped off the glove with a doorman. I felt another pang of conscience. I crossed the street to look at a shell of a building struck by a bomb in the Blitz. Its insides still stood bare and open, like a tree cut down by lightning.

We walked a few steps and LR stopped to sniff a doorway. I stood with my back toward the street, gazing into a watchmaker's shop. The sign read:

MASTER HUMPHREY'S CLOCK SHOP
CHARLES HUMPHREY,
PROUD PROPRIETOR SINCE 1894

A latticework of tape crisscrossed the store windows, to keep them from blowing out in big chunks in an explosion. But enough space had been left that you could see a dazzling display of antique timepieces.

I peered inside. An older man with a cane and a shock of white hair waved as he dusted a display. I smiled. He gestured to the tape and shrugged as if to say, "No matter what, I'm keeping my shop open."

He moved away but I kept looking at the watches. I loved how their faces shone like moons against their gold settings. Then, all at once, I felt a strange prickling again at the back of my neck. In the next instant, a sudden movement reflected in the glass caught my eye. I heard footsteps.

I froze, keeping my gaze on the window. The light captured the reflection of a man passing close behind me. He wore a black wool coat. His hands were stuck deep in his pockets; a newspaper was tucked under one arm. He had dark hair and wore no hat.

He could've been any man out for a stroll. But he seemed familiar somehow. Then I realized that I'd just seen him a few minutes before, reading a newspaper on a bench in Grosvenor Square. Still, it was more than that. There was something else. . . .

I stood still, my body half turned. I pretended to be studying each shiny timepiece with care. I waited, hoping to get a look at his face. And then he glanced at me—and down at Little Roo.

It was him. I knew it. This was the frowning young man from last night's raid—the one whose eyes had seemed to bore into me. Was he part of this mystery somehow? And could he be following us?

I wondered if he recognized me. Maybe not. Then one of those rules I'd read about for spies popped into my head: Always try to blend in. Little Roo. He would definitely remember LR. Even if London had been full of dogs—and it wasn't—she would *always* stand out.

At least there was something the man might *not* have noticed yesterday: the notebook. It had been at LR's feet, and her thick, furry paws would have hidden it.

Stop imagining things, I told myself. First I'd been concocting theories about George. Now I was making conjectures about a total stranger.

I had no evidence he had anything to do with the American girl or the woman on Mill Street. Yes, he'd come along Maddox Street a few minutes after the girl had rushed off. He might have been following her. It was even possible that he'd come out of Mill Street.

It's just a coincidence, I told myself. And at first I thought it was.

Little Roo and I kept walking. I didn't see the man for a few blocks. But then, near Hanover Square, I had that prickly sensation again and glanced over my shoulder.

And there he was, across the street—behind me.

My stomach fluttered. I felt a little queasy. Somehow, without my noticing, the man had stopped. Had he waited for me to catch up so he could get behind me?

I tugged at LR's lead and set off again, slowly now. I tried to piece the puzzle together in my mind and think how this man might fit into it. George had said there might be people willing to sell secrets to the Germans here. Even in London, there might be double agents.

Secrets. Secrets that might be hidden in code in the notebook. I wasn't sure how secret agents worked, but maybe the notebook contained important information.

My mind raced. Maybe the man had spotted the American girl and the young woman together, and now he was after the notebook. What if he'd knocked down the young woman? When he discovered she wasn't carrying the notebook, he might have set off after the girl.

She'd been running toward Grosvenor Square. Maybe, like me, he'd gone there today hoping to find her.

Or maybe, I thought, *it's all just in my mind.* Even so, it probably wasn't a good idea to go straight home. Not until I was sure he wasn't following me. I decided to wander somewhere else, keeping to crowded streets. It would be good to have a destination in mind, though. I tried to think of somewhere to go.

Baker Street. I'd head to 221 Baker Street. Sherlock Holmes had lived at 221B Baker Street, which, of course, didn't actually exist. But last summer, David and I had gone to where that address would have been. There was a bank there. And when we stepped inside, someone told us Sherlock Holmes got so many letters the bank employed a secretary to answer them.

I stopped for a moment. I bent down and ruffled LR's fur. "I can't be absolutely sure he's watching us. But if he is, we need to turn the tables."

LR looked up at me and cocked her head expectantly. I tried to remember the instructions on surveillance I'd read in the notebook. "Here's what we do, girl. First, we lose him. Next, we become the watchers. We make him our quarry, sort of the way you chase a squirrel."

Little Roo gave a sharp *woof!* Her nose started to twitch and she began looking around frantically in all directions. Oops! *Squirrel* might have been a bad example.

"Never mind," I told her, tugging her lead. "Let's just go."

CHAPTER EIGHT

If you suspect that you are being
watched . . . show no signs of suspicion.
—*SOE Manual*

Learning to be a spy isn't easy. You have to think about each and every detail. I tried to remember what I'd read about surveillance in the notebook that morning, especially the parts on what to do if you think you're being watched:

> Visit at least one crowded place.
> Do not go straight to your destination.
> Behave innocently and act naturally.

I could do that. I would take crowded main streets. By now it was Saturday afternoon. People were out shopping, waiting in queues with their ration books for meat or eggs or bread. It would be easy to keep to main roads and meander north to Baker Street instead of heading straight home. And as for the last point: What could be more innocent than a kid walking his dog?

Walking a dog allowed for all kinds of starts and stops. LR and I trotted along quickly for a few blocks. Then I stopped to let her sniff. In one small park, I found a stick and threw it for her a few times until she got bored. That took about two minutes. Even though she was a spaniel, LR wasn't much of a retriever.

After about twenty minutes, I was beginning to run out of ideas. Occasionally I stole a backward glance. The man was still trailing us, or at least he was still headed in the same direction.

I wished I'd read more of the training notes in the notebook. Maybe I should've brought it with me. That wouldn't have done much good, though. I mean, I couldn't exactly holler, "Hey, quarry. Can you stop while I read this next section?"

To become a real spy, I'd have to get better at memorizing. I needed to become more like my cousin Jeffrey, who was always bragging about the school prizes he won. That was one thing I liked about David. He was the smartest kid in our class, but he never made anyone else feel dumb.

And then, on Regent Street, I had some luck. A bus stopped beside us at the curb, and a crowd of people inched forward, shoulder to shoulder, ready to board and get home, out of the chilly air.

This is our chance! I realized. I snatched up LR and squeezed past, murmuring, "Pardon me." Soon there was a mass of heads and hats between the man and me.

When several pedestrians began to cross the road in

front of the stopped bus, I dashed out too. I stayed well hidden in the middle of the group, keeping up with a tall, broad gentleman. I walked so close to him he shot me a panicked look, as if he suspected I might be a pickpocket. Or maybe he didn't like dogs. I smiled and tucked LR under my old jacket.

Before, I'd been a boy walking a dog. Now if the man with the dark eyes tried to pick me out of the crowd, he wouldn't see the telltale furry legs of a spaniel anywhere.

Reaching the other side of the road, I pressed myself into a doorway. I looked across the street, standing on tiptoes. And there he was: ahead of us and on the other side. He hadn't seen us cross. We'd lost him!

"We did it, LR," I whispered. "If he *was* following us, I bet he thinks we got on that bus. If he's thinking about us at all. And now he's *our* quarry." I grinned to myself. "We can call him Q."

I felt rather pleased with myself. I was already becoming a spy.

I didn't have much time to stop and congratulate myself. I could easily lose Q in this crowd, and I was curious about where he might go. I turned my thoughts to the task at hand, trying to recall hints for being the watcher:

It is often better to use the opposite side of the road. Check. I was already doing this.

Keep something between yourself and the quarry. That meant I should try to stay behind other people. Easy, with all these shoppers out.

Note your quarry's features so you can recognize him again. I could do that too: I'd already gotten a good look at him. I'd noticed he had large ears and a high, sloping forehead. His nose was longish and his hair dark. It was his eyes you remembered—that clear, sharp stare. Still, it wouldn't be easy. Half the men in this part of London wore black coats and had dark hair.

LR squirmed in my arms, but I didn't let her down and take the chance of passersby wanting to stop and chat as they admired her long eyelashes and cute little snout.

I saw Q enter a store and come out again with a small parcel. At the next intersection, he changed directions, turning left on Oxford Street. After that, he headed north toward Portman Square and Baker Street.

We were now on Baker Street—exactly where I'd planned to go. A woman in front of me pushing a pram stopped short so she could adjust her baby's blanket. I tried to step around her. The woman cooed when she saw Little Roo in my arms. "Why, hullo, lovey. Isn't she a darling!"

Oh, no. Here we go. I smiled and said hastily, "Um, your baby is cute too. Have a nice day, now."

I sprinted around the pram and trotted along. I didn't want to lose Q after all this. I glanced across the street just in time to see him slip into what looked to be an office building.

Surprised, I stepped back, hiding in the doorway of a shop. I let Little Roo down so she could sniff at the sandbags that were piled up to prevent fire from spreading when bombs hit.

There didn't seem to be anything special about the building. It was made of gray stone, about six stories high. My eyes stayed glued to the windows. All at once, I spied the silhouette of a man's head in a second-floor window. I saw him glance outside, so I stepped back out of sight. When I looked again, he was gone. The window was dark. He must have drawn the blackout curtains even though it wasn't yet dusk.

It had all happened quickly, but I'd had time to recognize him. My quarry was in there. I waited five minutes, but no one came out. I decided to cross over for a closer look. It was numbered 64 Baker Street. A small plaque on the building read INTER-SERVICES RESEARCH BUREAU. I frowned. What in the world did that mean?

As LR and I stood there, a large, shiny black dog approached, pulling its owner toward the door. LR froze, but the other dog seemed more interested in going inside. It waved its thick black plume of a tail and nosed at the door, making a low whining sound.

Just as I'd done, the woman with the dog glanced curiously at the sign. "Aha," she murmured. "So this must be where he goes."

"Pardon me?" I said as LR tried to hide behind my legs.

At that moment, the door began to open. I snatched up Little Roo quickly and turned, walking a few paces away to gaze in the window of a shoe shop. I shot a quick glance behind me, keeping my face hidden. But it wasn't Q. This man was older.

"Julia, what are you doing here?" he said, his voice sharp.

"I could ask you the same question," she replied. I couldn't see her face, but I could hear the surprise in her voice. "What is this place?"

"Never mind that. But how did you find me?"

"I haven't been prying, if that's what you think. Hero led me right here," she said. "He knows the way, I guess, from you taking him to work."

I didn't wait to hear more. Ducking my head, I scurried off. At the next corner, I took a right on Dorset Street. I'd head back to Soho along quiet side streets.

"Maybe I *am* starting to think like a spy, LR," I said softly, stopping to let her down. "Because it sounded to me as if that man's wife didn't know where he works. Now, why wouldn't he tell her?"

I thought about it for all of a minute. The answer seemed clear: The Inter-Services Research Bureau must have something to do with the war.

And suddenly the words I'd read in the notebook that morning came back to me. "Sometimes SOE agents are called the Baker Street Irregulars, like the ragtag bunch of urchins Sherlock Holmes relied on to gather information. And, of course, our headquarters are there, though you wouldn't know it from the sign on the building."

Could the Inter-Services Research Bureau be a cover for the SOE, the Special Operations Executive?

I shivered and my stomach growled. It felt like I'd been on my feet for hours. Finally we turned onto Broadwick Street. I was about to enter Trenchard House when I heard footsteps come up rapidly behind me. Someone grabbed my arm, hard.

"Where is it?" a voice hissed in my ear. "I know you have it."

CHAPTER NINE

The watcher should always try to be one jump
ahead of the quarry.

—*SOE Manual*

I whirled around. My mouth fell open. "It's you!"

I recognized her blue coat. She carried a knapsack. She had straight brown hair that fell to her chin.

"Of course it's me." The American girl rolled her eyes, which were brown like LR's and almost as round. She didn't seem much friendlier than last night. "I've been following you, hoping you'd lead me to where you live." She stamped her foot. "Hand it over."

"What?" I said, trying to buy time. I'd just been so proud of myself for evading my quarry and tracking Q, or whatever his real name was, to Baker Street. All the while, this girl had been on my tail.

Some spy I was.

"You know what. The notebook, of course," she said, crossing her arms. "I'm positive I lost it right when you bumped into me. I'm sure it fell out of my pocket. You *must* have it."

I could hear desperation in her voice. *She doesn't know for sure,* I realized. "Well, first you need to tell me what's in it. That way I can be sure it really belongs to—"

"You do have it!" She cut me off.

I relented. "Yeah, I have it."

The girl stuck out her hand. "Then you can give it to me now."

"Uh, no. No, I can't." My answer surprised me almost as much as it did her.

"What do you mean, no?" she cried. "It isn't yours. It has nothing to do with you."

But it does, I thought. I couldn't hand it over without finding out the truth. I changed the subject. "Well, I'm curious. How did you track me here?"

"Believe me, it wasn't hard," she declared, hiding a small smile. "It wasn't quite dark last night. Flares and searchlights lit up the sky. And that made your hair glow. No wonder—it's almost as red as one of those phone booths. You're not exactly difficult to pick out in a crowd."

I really needed to wear a hat. I kept failing at blending in.

"And, of course, I recognized your dog." This time she did smile. I glanced down at LR, who was acting as if the girl was an old friend.

"It's not just that. As soon as I realized I'd lost the notebook, I suspected you had it," the girl went on. "Actually, I thought they might know you at the Mayfair air-raid command post. I was on my way there, but then I spotted you and your dog in Grosvenor Square." She shrugged. "The rest was easy."

Easy! I didn't feel as if I'd had an easy afternoon following Q.

LR jumped up on the girl's legs. The girl bent down and petted her head. "Nice to see you again. What's her name?"

"It's Roo, like Kanga's baby in *Winnie-the-Pooh*. Only she's a girl. Her first owner was a children's librarian," I explained. "We call her Little Roo—LR for short."

I sighed. I loved my dog, even if she was rather silly-looking and didn't have a solemn, distinguished name like Hero. But having a cute dog was definitely making this spy business a lot harder. What was that other rule? Don't carry any conspicuous items.

"Well, even though you did zig and zag a lot today, I could usually spot Little Roo trotting along at your heels," the girl was saying. "I saw you stop in front of a building on Baker Street. I thought you might live there, but then you took off and came here."

The girl's words sank in. I almost gasped aloud. *She doesn't know about Q!* I realized. She'd tracked LR and me, but never noticed *my* quarry.

The girl moved to stand in front of me, blocking my

way into Trenchard House. Her voice sounded serious again. "Listen, this looks like a police station. I . . . I can't let you give the notebook to the police."

"I'm not going to do that."

"Then what are you doing here?"

"Uh, well, actually I live here," I admitted.

"Really?" Her eyebrows shot up. "In a police station? So is your room a cell?"

"It's not like that." Since we'd been standing in front of Trenchard House, several young constables had come and gone. "It's a boardinghouse for single policemen," I explained. "My dad is a police sergeant and also the resident caretaker."

"Have you told him about the notebook?"

I shook my head. "No. I haven't told anyone." That was true. I'd asked David for help with secret codes, but I hadn't said anything about the notebook.

Jimmy Wilson sauntered by. "Hullo, Bertie. Enjoying your afternoon?" I waved. He winked and peered curiously at the American girl before entering Trenchard House.

"So that's your name: Bertie?" she asked.

"Yes. I'm Bertie Bradshaw."

"Well, Bertie Bradshaw, I'm getting tired of waiting. Do you have it with you?"

"I wouldn't carry something like that around," I told her. "Listen, I promise I'll give it to you, but . . . but I just want to be absolutely sure it's yours. There's a little park called Golden Square close by. We can talk there."

She bit her lip. I half expected her to try to reach into my pockets or run into Trenchard House and break down the door of my flat to get the notebook. Also, I wanted to leave before anyone else came by, like George Morton. I knew I'd get teased for talking to a girl.

More than anything, I wanted more time to think.

Because if the American girl hadn't noticed I was following Q, that confirmed my suspicion: She was too young to be a secret agent.

This girl hadn't been to spy school. The notebook didn't belong to her at all. But I had a feeling she knew whose it was. And I wanted to find out.

PART TWO

The Game Is Afoot

Come, Watson, come! . . . The game is afoot.
—Sherlock Holmes,
in "The Adventure of the Abbey Grange"

Spy Practice Number Two

CAESAR (SHIFT) CIPHER

kagwz aiyky qftap eimfe azetq dxaow taxyq e

This type of substitution cipher is called a Caesar cipher, named for Roman emperor Julius Caesar, who liked to use it in his letters. It's also called a shift cipher. Once you find the answer to the clue, write out the regular alphabet. Then, starting on *A*, count that number of places to the right (don't include *A* itself in the number). The letter you land on becomes the first letter in your cipher alphabet.

For example, say the clue is to add the month and date of Independence Day. You add seven (since July is the seventh month) and four (for July fourth), making a total shift of eleven. So you shift the alphabet eleven letters to the right. *A* becomes *L* in your cipher alphabet, *B* becomes *M*, and so on. Here's a table to help you:

PLAIN	A	B	C	D	E	F	G	H	I	J	K	L	M	N	O	P	Q	R	S	T	U	V	W	X	Y	Z
CIPHER	L	M	N	O	P	Q	R	S	T	U	V	W	X	Y	Z	A	B	C	D	E	F	G	H	I	J	K

Hint: To decode this message, use a shift that's equal to the number of the month plus the date on which Operation Neptune (the code name for the D-Day landings in France) took place. Once again, you can research the date of D-Day in this book, in another book, or online.

You'll notice there are no spaces between the letters in the cipher message to help you guess at the words. That's on purpose. It makes it a little harder to figure out.

CHAPTER TEN

It seemed to me as I walked through the brick compartments of that shelter that I learned something about fear, and the resistance to total destruction which exists in all human beings.

—Eleanor Roosevelt on her visit to London, in her column My Day, October 27, 1942

"You know my name, so what's yours?" I asked as we made our way through the narrow streets toward Golden Square.

"It's Eleanor. Eleanor Shea."

"Like Eleanor Roosevelt, the First Lady?"

"Yes, I was even named for her."

I glanced over. Eleanor was about my height. She couldn't be old enough to be a spy. "So, um, are you about twelve?"

"No," she cried indignantly. "I was thirteen in July. I have a patriotic birthday: the Fourth of July. And just so you know, I always go by Eleanor. Not Ellie or Ella or Nell. Always Eleanor."

"Whatever you say, Always Eleanor."

Eleanor flashed a quick smile, but it didn't last long. "Bertie, I'm sorry if I was a little rude back there. Father says I sometimes barrel over people like a runaway train. But when I got home last night and realized I'd lost the notebook, I blamed myself. I couldn't sleep."

I felt a little sorry for her then. I knew what it was like to stare at the ceiling and toss and turn.

"Hey, I've got to stop and tie my shoelace," I said. "Would you mind holding Little Roo's lead for me?"

"Sure! I love animals," Eleanor replied. "Cats especially, but dogs too. Nan has a cat named Beatrix after Beatrix Potter. You know, she—"

"I know who she was," I broke in. "I'm English, remember? I grew up on Peter Rabbit."

I glanced down at LR. It could've been worse. She might have been named after one of those bunnies. Probably Mopsy.

We were silent until we reached Golden Square. It was time to get down to business.

"Listen," I said as we sat on a bench. I took back LR's lead, and she settled at my feet. "I understand why you were upset about losing the notebook. Especially after I read some of it."

"You read it?" Eleanor bristled. "But . . . you had no right to do that."

"I didn't plan to," I admitted. "At first I was just trying to find a name inside. Once I realized what it was about, I couldn't *stop* reading it."

Eleanor bit her lip but said nothing. I was almost sure now: She hadn't read it herself. *She has no idea what's in it,* I realized.

A few pigeons perched on the head of the statue of King George II. LR sniffed around under the bench, hunting for crumbs.

I took a breath. "Eleanor, I know you dropped the notebook. But that doesn't make it yours. Who does it really belong to?"

Eleanor dug her hands in her coat pockets. I could tell she didn't want to answer me. "Why . . . why should I tell you?" She didn't look at me. I felt like I was skirting too close to something she didn't want to talk about.

"Well, maybe I could help find that person," I offered. "That is, if you needed help."

Eleanor said nothing. I thought of something Dad had told me when I was trying to teach Little Roo to fetch a ball. "If you want her to drop it, don't go prying it out of her mouth. That'll make her bite down on it tenaciously. Just go about it easy like."

I tried to back off and act like I didn't really care. I shrugged. "But maybe you don't need any help. It just seems fair that you should tell me a little. I mean, if it wasn't for me, you might have lost it completely."

"If it wasn't for you, I would never have lost it."

I was trying to think of what to say next when Eleanor let out a deep breath. "Oh, all right, you seem like you're an honest person. I guess you have to be, living in a police station."

I wasn't so sure about that.

"You guessed right," she went on. "It isn't my notebook. But . . . but that's all I can tell you."

I said slowly, "I know the notebook is important. That's why I don't have it with me. You haven't read it yourself, have you?"

"No," Eleanor admitted. "I haven't. There wasn't . . . that is, someone asked me to keep it for a while. To keep it safe until . . ."

"Until what?"

She spoke slowly, as if she was trying to choose her words carefully. "Until the owner wants it back."

I pressed ahead. "Did the owner give it to you yesterday—just before the air raid?"

Eleanor shot me a startled glance. "Hold on. There's no way you could . . ."

"Eleanor, does the notebook belong to a young woman with dark hair?"

"I don't understand," Eleanor said in a hoarse whisper. "How could you possibly know that?"

"I know because I saw her last night, after you ran off."

"You talked to her?"

I shook my head. "No, not exactly."

"Then how did you guess it was hers? I don't understand."

"Well, LR found the notebook and I stuck it in my pocket after you left," I began. "But then Little Roo took off running. She led me back to a small side street right off of Maddox—more like an alleyway, really."

"And then what?"

I was almost afraid to say it aloud. "When . . . when I got there, I found a young woman."

"What did she say?"

"She didn't say anything. She was on the ground," I said slowly. "Maybe she fell. I don't know. But I couldn't ask her anything. Don't worry—she wasn't dead," I added hastily. "But . . . she was unconscious."

"Unconscious!" Eleanor echoed. "Is she all right now? Where is she?"

"That's the thing. You see, I put my coat over her. Then I rode my bicycle to the command post to get help," I said. "When we came back . . . she was gone."

"Gone." Eleanor stared at me. "Oh, I'm so confused. What happened to her?"

"I don't know. I even went back to Mill Street this morning to look for clues. I guess it's possible she got up and left," I said. "Eleanor, it might help if you tell me who she was."

Eleanor shook her head.

I tried again. "Is she your sister?"

"No, she's not my sister."

There was a long pause. I thought she might not tell me. At last Eleanor seemed to make up her mind. She heaved a sigh, as if she'd been holding her breath. "All right. I'll tell you, but you have to promise not to tell anyone else."

"I promise."

"Well, her name is Violette Romy. She's about

twenty-three. Violette was my French tutor last year. She left last spring and I hadn't heard from her in months."

French tutor . . . I remembered something from the notebook. The person was being trained to go into the field—into another country. A country occupied by the Nazis. Could it be France?

"Violette was originally from France, wasn't she?" I recalled how the writer had used the French word *maman* for "mama" in the notebook.

Eleanor nodded. "Yes, she was born in Paris. She was an only child. She never talked about her father. But after her mother died, Violette came to London. My father hired her to help me because when we arrived I was so behind in French compared to the other girls in my class."

"Did you know Violette well?"

Eleanor nodded. "We met twice a week. I'm an only child too. And I was lonely, especially when we first came. Violette is . . . well, she's my friend. I'd do almost anything to help her."

"When did you see Violette again, after she stopped being your tutor?" I asked. I was trying to piece together the story. If Violette had trained to be an agent in France, why had she come back? And why had she given Eleanor her secret notebook?

"I hadn't seen her for months until yesterday," Eleanor explained. "In the morning, I found a note pushed under our door. Violette asked me to meet her in the afternoon. I was so excited! We met up and made our way to Regent Street and went window-shopping. But Violette seemed different somehow." Eleanor got up and began pacing back and forth.

"How different?"

"Well, her looks, for one thing. Violette was always neat and stylish. Yesterday she seemed thinner; her clothes were worn. And she acted strange." Eleanor's words spilled out.

I frowned. "What do you mean?"

"Well, I thought we'd catch up and maybe go have tea together. But Violette seemed preoccupied. She didn't ask me many questions about what I've been doing. And when I tried to find out where she'd been, she wouldn't really say. She just changed the subject."

"Did you just walk along Regent Street?"

Eleanor nodded. She closed her eyes for a second, as if she was trying to replay the events in her mind. "Violette kept looking around, here and there and sometimes over her shoulder. We'd stand in front of one window, and then she'd want to race across the street to see something else."

I drew in a breath.

"What?" Eleanor asked.

"Nothing."

But was it nothing? Maybe Violette had been practicing a strategy from her notebook, just as I'd done today while trailing my quarry: It is often better to use the opposite side of the road. Had Violette been following someone? Or had she been worried about *being* followed? We were quiet for a few minutes. "Eleanor, what did Violette say when she gave you the notebook?"

"Well, it was getting late. I told her I needed to get home to my grandmother. My father and I live with her, you see," Eleanor explained. "And that's when Violette said she had something she wanted me to keep for her, just for a week or so. She came close and slipped the notebook into my coat pocket."

"She didn't tell you what was in it?"

"No. But she said she wanted to trust me with something important." Eleanor paused and glanced around. "Then Violette murmured, 'Thursday evening. I've set the trap for then. Please just keep this for me . . . just in case. If you don't hear from me by Friday, if not before, then . . . '"

"Then what?" I cried, eager to hear the rest. I wondered what kind of trap Violette had set. And could she still follow through with it, or had someone stopped her?

I shivered, and it wasn't just because I'd gotten cold sitting on the bench. I asked again, "And then what?"

Eleanor sank back down beside me. "That's when the sirens started wailing. There were so many people, jostling and pushing. We got separated. I wanted to get home to Nan. That's where I was heading when you ran into me.

"I don't know what to think," she added. "Bertie,

you've read parts of the notebook. Does it explain what Violette has been doing all these months?"

"Yes, I think so." I wondered if Eleanor would be shocked. "I think Violette stopped being your tutor to train as a secret agent."

Eleanor was less surprised than I'd expected. She cocked her head and considered the idea. "Do you mean she might be working as an agent here in London?"

I shook my head. "No. At least I'm not sure. I think it was probably in a country in Europe, occupied by the Nazis. I guess we can assume it was France, since she spoke French. But that's not all." I lowered my voice, though there was no one near us. "I didn't read the entire notebook, so there's a lot I don't know. But the last pages are filled with strings of letters—letters that don't make any sense at all. Gibberish."

"Gibberish," she repeated. "You mean like it's in some sort of code?"

I nodded. "Yes. Exactly like that."

"And now Violette is missing. She could be hurt, or kidnapped. I'm afraid she's in some sort of trouble, Bertie." Eleanor clenched her fists. "If only we had more clues to what happened to her."

"She might be safe. She might have just walked home. Did she say where she was living?" I asked. "With a friend, or did she have a flat? Or maybe she was staying in a hotel?"

Eleanor shook her head. "I know Violette used to

live alone in a small rented room. I don't know exactly where it was, though. And now . . . now I have no idea."

"So there's no way to check if she reached home last night." I frowned. That would make finding her hard, if not impossible. I had another thought—if Violette was renting a room in a boardinghouse or a hotel, she might not even have used her real name.

Eleanor sighed and turned to face me. "I guess, after all, it's a good thing you ran me down, Bertie. Because if I hadn't met you and dropped the notebook, I'd never know something might have happened to Violette.

"But if something *has* happened, then whatever plan Violette set in motion for Thursday might be ruined. That's only five days from now. . . ." Her voice trailed off.

"But we can help." I leaned forward. "We can figure out what the trap is and be there in Violette's place. I know we can do it. Let me help."

Eleanor opened her mouth to answer. At that moment, the air was split by the eerie, spine-chilling rise and fall of the warning sirens. LR started to quiver. She lifted up her small snout and wailed, *Wooo . . . wooo*. It was happening again.

CHAPTER ELEVEN

The agent should merge into the background
and act in the same way as those around him.
                                    —SOE Manual

The air-raid siren made me bolt to my feet. "It hasn't
even been twenty-four hours since the last bombing
raid," I cried. "I'm on call tonight. I need to go home to
get my bicycle. And my helmet."

"Let me take Little Roo," Eleanor offered. "I know
where the Mayfair command post is. We can run and
meet you there. That will save you time."

"But . . ."

"It'll be fine. She likes me." Eleanor grabbed LR's
lead. "It's not like I'm going to steal her."

I hesitated, but only for a second. I couldn't afford to
be late again, and I could ride faster without LR in the
basket. "All right. Once I get my bike, it'll take me less
than five minutes to reach the command post."

"Let's go, Little Roo!" And Eleanor was off, LR trotting behind her.

The flat was empty; Dad wasn't back. I pulled on my helmet and grabbed my torch. I pulled down the black-out shade in the kitchen, so if Dad came in and turned on a light, it wouldn't shine outside. I was halfway out the door when I remembered to stop and scribble a quick note.

Jimmy was at the reception desk. All the constables had to take turns answering the phone on weekends. I called out, "Missing the Saturday dance tonight?"

"Not a chance." Jimmy flashed a wide smile. "I asked George to take over my shift later. He doesn't care about dancing. I hope the raid ends in time. If you were a bit older, you could bring your little friend. Now, haven't I seen her before?"

"I don't think so. Well, I'm off."

He waved me on. "Be careful, Bertie."

This time will be different, I vowed, pedaling hard. *This time I'll make the wardens proud of me.* Dusk was falling and my stomach growled. I hadn't eaten anything since breakfast.

The air-raid sirens blared, their awful voices rising and falling in that eerie, urgent wail. People scurried along the streets, heading home to their Morrison shelters or to Anderson shelters in their gardens. Others made their way to public shelters or Tube stations.

When I rushed into the command post, Warden

Ita greeted me with a warm smile. "Ah, Bertie. You've made good time and I see you've got your helmet on. And you arranged for our Miss Shea to bring your rescue dog."

Our Miss Shea? "You . . . you know Eleanor?"

"A little. She volunteers with the PDSA, the People's Dispensary for Sick Animals. You know, the folks that rescue animals from bombed-out houses. We coordinate with them quite a bit."

"Where is she now?" I asked. "And where's LR?"

"I've just sent them out to an incident." The phone on the desk jangled sharply. Warden Ita held up his hand. "Hold on a minute."

He answered the phone and took a few notes. "Got it. Thank you." Then he turned back to me. "That was the ambulance station," Warden Ita said. "Here's what I need you to do. A house on Berkeley Square was hit. Let the rescue team know there'll be a short delay but the ambulance will arrive as soon as possible."

"Yes, sir. I can be there in two or three minutes." It was less than half a mile away.

"I'll come and check on the situation when I can. Watch out for delayed-action bombs and incendiaries," Warden Ita warned. Incendiary bombs, I knew, could cause destructive fires. Everyone in London remembered December 29, 1940, when the magnificent St. Paul's Cathedral had been saved by dedicated fire watchers.

It felt strange to be riding my bicycle without Little Roo's ears flapping in the breeze in front of me. I could hear the rumbling drone of planes and the ack-ack fire sputtering around me. Anti-aircraft guns, all trained skyward, were stationed throughout the city.

I hoped this raid would be short, like the one last night. In the Blitz, all-night raids hadn't kept ambulance drivers, fire watchers, air-raid wardens, and rescue volunteers from their duties. They'd saved people from the rubble, fought fires, and rushed the wounded to hospitals. Some had been killed.

At least tonight I had my helmet.

It was easy to see where the bomb had hit. One corner of a two-story house had been blown away. Dust and smoke still filled the air.

I threw down my bicycle and Eleanor came running toward me, wearing a tin helmet with PDSA RESCUE stenciled on it. She must have been carrying it in her knapsack all day. Eleanor was better prepared than I was.

"Where's Little Roo?"

"Oh, Bertie, the rescue team needed her." Eleanor's cheeks were flushed red from running and the cold air. "Two small children on the first floor are trapped inside with their mother." She touched my arm as we hurried toward the building. "I'm sorry. I wanted to wait until you got here. But you should've seen Little Roo! She really wanted to help. And everyone says the heavy rescue men are the best. They work in construction and know how houses are put together."

I swallowed hard. "I wish I'd been here. She's just . . . she's so little."

We got as close as we could; then the waiting began. The minutes seemed endless. Ten . . . fifteen . . . twenty. The all clear sounded. After that, a crowd began to gather. Neighbors emerged from nearby houses, or stopped to look as they returned home from shelters.

People huddled close in the cold and spoke in whispers. Silence was important: The rescue workers had to listen for sounds from survivors. We all waited for a whimper, a cry, an excited shout that meant someone had been found alive.

"The man who took Little Roo inside said she was a silly-looking thing. But I stood up for her," Eleanor whispered. "I said LR was as good as Rip and Rex, those famous rescue dogs from the Blitz. We learned about them in my PDSA training." She patted my arm awkwardly. "Sorry, Bertie. I talk a lot when I'm nervous."

"It's all right." I dug my fingernails into my palms. My stomach was a mass of knots. I stood on tiptoes and tried to peer into the hole where the front door had been. "Where do they think the children are?"

"I heard a neighbor say the family has a Morrison shelter in the kitchen," Eleanor said softly. "I guess the problem is getting them out without more of the building collapsing."

Somewhere inside, a man shouted, "Watch out there!"

Then we heard a piercing yelp of pain.

CHAPTER TWELVE

Undaunted by smouldering debris, thick
smoke, intense heat and jets of water from
fire hoses, this dog displayed uncanny
intelligence and outstanding determination in
his efforts to follow up any scent which led
him to a trapped casualty.

—PDSA Dickin Medal citation for Rex,
civil defense rescue dog

"Little Roo!" I leaped forward.

Eleanor grabbed my arm. "We have to stay back. They'll bring her out. You'll see."

I shook her off and plunged ahead. I didn't get far. A burly rescue worker in dark blue overalls stood in the entrance with a lantern. He put out his arm. "Easy now, lad. We don't want anyone else to get hurt."

I stepped back, my eyes glued to the gaping hole where a door had been. Through it, I could see smashed furniture, a broken pram, a child's boot. The family had probably gone for a walk that very afternoon. I imagined a young mother, waiting in a long queue with her ration card to buy food for her family.

And now . . . I swallowed hard. I knew that a dog, even a dog helping in a rescue, would always be last on the list to save.

"How are things going?" Warden Ita asked softly. He'd come up behind us. His arm on my shoulder felt solid and warm.

"Hello, Warden." The rescue worker shifted his hurricane lamp so he could shake hands. "We're trying to get two little ones and their mum out. The spaniel helped us find a path to them. But now it seems as if some of the rubble has shifted."

"Any injuries?" Warden Ita gestured toward the street. "The ambulance has just arrived. We'll keep it standing by."

"Can't be sure yet," the rescue worker replied. He wiped brick dust from his eyes, leaving a smudge on his broad face. "You know, Warden, I thought we were done with all this. I'm not sure how much longer Londoners can hold out."

"We'll hold out as long as we must," Warden Ita assured him. "Besides, the tide's turning. Once our troops invade France, they'll drive Hitler's forces back to Berlin in no time."

The man asked a question about the rescue worker schedule, and Warden Ita moved closer to answer. I felt cold suddenly, without him behind me. I couldn't hear their exact words, but a strange thing happened. Their voices started to sound distant and tinny.

Maybe I was just hungry, but I started to feel dizzy, and hot and cold at the same time. One minute it was like being stuck at the bottom of an empty well. And then it seemed like someone was pouring icy water in over my head. The water got deeper and deeper, creeping over my chin and up to my mouth. I had a hard time catching my breath.

Images flooded in. I was there again. Our old house. I could smell the sharp cordite of the gunpowder, the burning wood. Thick brick dust clogged my throat and nostrils. The sounds came back too. The staccato of the ack-ack guns, rumbling planes, walls and beams crashing.

Terrified screams. My screams.

One part of me knew it wasn't real. I tried counting. That had worked before. *One two three. One two three.* Then I felt myself sway and was sure I'd be sick to my stomach.

"Bertie!" I heard my name and felt someone grab me hard. "Bertie!"

I opened my eyes. And there was Dad. He pushed my head down close to my knees. "Keep your head down, lad, before you faint. Breathe now. Slow and easy. That's it. You're all right, son. It's going to be all right."

Ten minutes later, I was able to stand up straight without the world spinning.

Eleanor stood beside me, closer now. She didn't say anything. But she did push a doughnut into my hand. I mumbled my thanks and nibbled gratefully.

After a while, Eleanor reached across me to shake my father's hand. "Good evening, Officer Bradshaw, you must be Bertie's father. I'm Eleanor Shea. Bertie and I volunteer together."

We do? I thought. I shot her a glance but she was smiling politely at Dad.

At that moment, we heard a shout from inside. The burly heavy rescue man who'd been talking to Warden Ita disappeared into the rubble carrying some rope.

He returned shortly, saying, "We've got our best team in there: Stan's a stubborn Scotsman and Tommy never gives up. But it's slow going. They don't want to disturb anything and bring beams crashing down."

I swallowed hard. "We heard Roo yelp," I told Dad. "I just hope she's not hurt."

He squeezed my shoulder. "Oh, she's tough. She'll want to be getting home for her tea."

"How was your afternoon?" I managed to ask. My shivering had stopped, along with the strange queasy feeling. But Dad kept his arm around my shoulder.

"Fine. Will's spirits are fine. The doctors are good and everything's going as well as we can expect," he said.

"How did you find me here?" I asked.

"After I got your note, I decided to check in at the command post. I saw Warden Hawk, who directed me here. Just hold on a little longer, Bertie. They're doing their best to bring everyone out."

Neighbors still huddled in small, anxious groups.

Some wore their nightclothes and shivered in the cold moonlight. During the Blitz, we'd all wandered the streets in pajamas with coats on top—even grown-ups. Some people would head to the Tube stations or public shelters each evening, prepared for a long night. And then they'd go home the next morning. After air-raid nights, school often didn't start until ten.

I'd had red pajamas then. Now I had blue ones. If I left them on my bed in the morning, I'd come home from school to find that Little Roo had scooped them up into a little nest. I'd seen her do it: She'd push them round and round with her paw. Then, when she was satisfied, she'd plopped down in just the perfect spot.

"'Ere's Tommy now!" cried the rescue volunteer.

A man covered in dirt and dust emerged, struggling to hold a baby girl in one arm and a squirming toddler in the other. Warden Ita sprang forward to take the little boy. He passed him back to one of the waiting ambulance women.

"Mummy!" the boy yelled between sobs. "I want Mummy."

A woman's voice answered, "I'm here, sweetheart. Right behind you."

The second rescue worker appeared, propping up a limping woman with one arm. This must be Stan. In his other arm, he held another squirming bundle. He grinned and called out, "And who belongs tae this furry creature?"

"Me!" I reached out to gather LR into my arms. "Is she all right?"

"Jist a wee cut on her front foot." He grinned as neighbors rushed forward to help the mother toward the ambulance. "Funny-looking thing. But she wouldna give up till she found th' wee bairns."

"Oh, thank you," I cried. LR's tail wagged crazily. She snuffled, licked my face, and buried her muzzle under my chin. She was warm and soft and alive. I felt her paw. "It seems all right. I'll check it when we get home."

"Go on, then, Bertie. Good job tonight—both of you," Warden Ita said. He nodded toward the American girl. "Best walk Eleanor home first."

I glanced at Dad.

"If you're up to it, go ahead, Bertie. I'll have tea and toast waiting for you. I'll find the first-aid kit too," he said. "Do you want me to take Little Roo home now?"

Dad looked at me and grinned so wide his mustache quivered. This morning he'd practically threatened to get rid of LR if I didn't start becoming more responsible. Now I wondered if he really would. Little Roo had wormed her way into his heart.

I smiled back. "That's all right, Dad. I'll walk my bike and LR can ride in the basket in case her paw hurts."

"Good night, Warden Ita." Eleanor shook his hand. "Also, may we ask a favor? Bertie needs me to help him out with a project. I wonder if we could use that small meeting room in the command post after school this week."

It was all I could do to keep my jaw from dropping open. *What is she talking about?*

"Of course," Warden Ita replied. "We have a regular meeting there on Tuesday afternoons, but other than that, it's fine. What are you helping Bertie with?"

I stared, wondering what she would say. But Eleanor was quick on her feet with an answer. "Oh, it's about books," she said smoothly. "My father's a literature professor back home in Connecticut. He's taught me a lot."

Dad's faced brightened. "Is your father teaching here in London?"

"Um . . . no. He works for the Office of Strategic Services." She shrugged. "Something to do with the war."

The Office of Strategic Services. What is that? I wondered. Like the Inter-Services Research Bureau, it seemed like a made-up name, meant to cover something else.

It occurred to me then that even if Eleanor Shea wasn't a spy, her father might be.

CHAPTER THIRTEEN

The agent should not . . . tell people more
than they need know, no matter how important
or close the association.

—*SOE Manual*

"This is so nice of you, Bertie. I don't live far. Just a little ways past Berkeley Square," said Eleanor as we set out.

I scowled. "Speaking of nice, that was a nasty trick you just played, Eleanor."

"What?" I could see her mouth quivering.

"It's not funny. You set up that whole arrangement with Warden Ita without asking me," I said. "Warden Ita already thinks I'm dim and forgetful. And he's the nice one, compared to Warden Hawk. The only reason Warden Hawk puts up with me is that he likes LR."

"Sorry about that." Eleanor reached over and tugged gently on one of LR's ears. "Everyone likes you, don't they, Roo? Well, Bertie, I had to think fast. Because I've made a decision."

"What's that?" I asked skeptically.

"I've decided to trust you."

"Thanks, I guess. But what does that even mean?"

"Well, you still haven't given me back the notebook. But remember, you can't tell anyone else about it, or turn it in to your father or a warden."

"I already told you I wouldn't."

"I know. But you do live in a police station, after all."

"I told you. It's *not* a police station!"

"You're so easy to tease, Bertie." Eleanor grinned. "And I'm sorry for barging ahead with that story about you needing help at school. You just looked so far away. Your face went all white. I thought making you mad might distract you from whatever it was that upset you."

"I can't talk about that," I muttered.

"You don't have to. I won't ask you anything personal," she said. "We don't even have to be friends. I'm not that good at being friends, anyway."

"I'm not either," I admitted. Except with David.

"But . . . well, it's like what we were saying before the raid tonight," Eleanor began. "Maybe the reason Violette was setting a trap is revealed somewhere in the notebook. Probably in the secret code. We have to at least *try* to figure it out."

"All right. We can be partners—like Sherlock Holmes and Dr. Watson," I said. "I'll be Sherlock."

"No way," cried Eleanor. "I want to be Sherlock."

LR erupted. *Woof! Woof!*

I grinned. "Little Roo wants to be Sherlock too, I

guess." I tickled her curly head and turned to Eleanor. "My dad's been a policeman for a long time. He's not a real detective inspector or anything. But he says it's important to trust your partner. You don't need to worry about me turning the notebook in."

"And you won't tell anyone else about this?"

"No, I won't. I promise." And I wouldn't.

But the truth was that I hadn't told her everything. I hadn't told her that I'd asked David for help with ciphers. I also hadn't revealed that I'd followed my quarry—the man I called Q—to Baker Street. I wasn't quite sure why I was holding back. But I couldn't help it: One tiny suspicion kept nagging at me.

I couldn't help thinking Q was up to no good. I mean, I'd seen him the night Violette had disappeared. But there was another possibility too. If Q was working at the Inter-Services Research Bureau and was after Violette, then maybe he'd been following Violette because *she* was up to no good.

I wasn't sure of anything.

Just as we turned down Hay's Mews, I stopped abruptly. Like Mill Street, this was an old, narrow passageway. I was lost in thought about Q. Just the notion that he might be lurking in the shadows made me shiver.

"What? Why do you keep looking over your shoulder?" Eleanor whispered.

"It's nothing." *There's no way he followed me back to Broadwick Street*, I reminded myself. *I'm positive he didn't even realize I trailed him to Baker Street.*

Eleanor pointed at a two-story building. "My room's over that archway. There are some fancy houses around us in Mayfair. But Nan lives in what once was a stable. Oh!" She dug into a side pocket of her knapsack and pulled out something wrapped in a napkin. "I just remembered I have one more doughnut. It's a little squished."

Rrrr . . . ruff! LR had been resting her chin on the rim of the bike basket. Now she sat up, wagging her tail at high speed.

"She knows she deserves a treat," Eleanor remarked. "I always get them from the ladies at the mobile American Red Cross carts."

She broke the doughnut in three pieces. LR lunged forward and grabbed one with her sharp little teeth.

"Hey, you be gentle!" I scolded.

"She's hungry, poor thing. She worked hard tonight. Is it hard to feed her because of all the food being rationed?" Eleanor asked. She pointed to a "Food Waste for Pigs" bin on the street corner. "I see these everywhere. But can you get dog food now?"

"No, she eats what we eat," I said. "Not that we have leftovers. At the beginning, a lot of people killed their pets because the government told them to do it. The London Zoo killed their poisonous snakes too, in case they got loose after a bombing raid."

"Poor snakes!" Eleanor rubbed noses with LR. "Well, I'm glad you're here, Roo."

"Me too," I said. "Whenever I take her for a walk, people are always stopping to pet her and share their stories."

Just last week, a man had stopped me and spent ten minutes telling me all about his old cat, Sophie. "She was mean, but we loved her." Another woman had almost cried, talking about her dog. "We gave our lovely Michael to the military; we couldn't afford to feed him. He's serving our country, but I'm afraid we'll never set eyes on him again."

Eleanor turned to say goodbye. "I'm glad you ran into me, Bertie Bradshaw. I'll see you Monday after school at the command post. Bring the notebook."

"I will. Good night, Always Eleanor."

Eleanor smiled. "Good night, Watson."

And then she ran inside.

CHAPTER FOURTEEN

Surveillance is the keeping of someone under
observation without his [or her] knowledge.

                                        —*SOE Manual*

SUNDAY

It was late morning, and my history book lay on the
floor, discarded. Who cared about Emperor Claudius
and the Romans invading England in AD 43? I was
more worried about Hitler.

Instead, I fished out Violette's notebook from under
Will's mattress and starting reading. LR was draped over
my feet, keeping them warm. Every few minutes, she
emitted funny snuffs and snores and wheezes. Sometimes her paws moved, like she was dreaming about her
rescue last night.

When I heard voices in the kitchen, I thought at
first it was a constable stopping by with a question for
Dad—something that happened a lot. A few minutes

later, my door burst open. I barely had time to thrust the notebook under the blanket before my cousin Jeffrey strode in.

He jumped on the foot of my bed and scooped up Little Roo. "Hey, little sweetheart. I hear you saved some children yesterday." Jeffrey turned to me and pushed a lock of blond hair from his eyes. "Wake up, lazy! Little Roo is the one who did the hard work."

"I'm not asleep," I grumbled. I pushed the notebook deeper under the covers.

"Your dad told me all about it," Jeffrey went on, gently examining LR's feet, which were sometimes hard to find under her thick fur. "He said her paw is fine, and she's not even limping. So that's good."

LR started sniffing Jeffrey's pocket and he laughed. "No fooling you, is there? I saved this biscuit I got on the train this morning just for you." Jeffrey grinned at me. "She loves me more than you do, Bertie."

"She doesn't know any better," I grumbled.

But it was true. LR adored Jeffrey. It was hard for me to feel the same. Jeffrey was a year older and a head taller than me. He was good at everything he tried, from sports to school. Jeffrey was *perfect*. Especially if you asked his mother, my aunt Mildred.

"Why are you here, anyway?" I asked him.

"Mother needed to come to town to do some shopping. I decided to tag along," said Jeffrey. "Come on, Bertie. Let's walk over to Grosvenor Square. Maybe we'll see some American generals."

On Broadwick Street, we ran into Jimmy and George returning from a shift. Jeffrey had met them on other visits and greeted them politely. That was another thing about Jeffrey. According to Aunt Mildred, he'd had excellent manners from the time he was two.

"Nice to see you again, Jeffrey," Jimmy was saying. "Now, aren't you at Strand School?"

"Yes, my grandmother is in the same town, so my mother and I are living with her. And it's near . . ." Jeffrey glanced at me. "Bertie's brother and mum are in Surrey now too, for Will's treatment. We're also close to a huge encampment of American soldiers. My friends and I go there all the time. The soldiers let us try on their helmets. They even tell us about the invasion." Jeffrey's blue eyes sparkled. "It's the biggest secret ever. Everyone is bursting to find out where and when it will be."

While Jimmy and George asked more questions about the American troops, I drifted away, letting LR pull me along to sniff interesting things. Well, they were interesting to *her*, at least.

"Let's go," said Jeffrey, coming up behind me a minute later. He turned and watched as the two constables went into Trenchard House. "You know, I hate to say this, but I don't much like him. I can't tell you exactly why."

I nodded, surprised we agreed on something. "I know what you mean. I think he's just so bitter about his scars."

"Oh, I didn't mean George. I was talking about the other one. Jimmy."

"Jimmy?" I asked. "What are you talking about? He's nice."

Jeffrey shrugged. "Like I said, I can't tell you exactly. But LR feels the same way. Haven't you noticed? She moves off or hides behind your legs when he's nearby. And we already know Little Roo is a better judge of character than you, Bertie."

I scowled. "I hope your school doesn't come back to London anytime soon, cousin."

"Aw, you know you miss me, Bertie Wertie." I scowled at the old nickname. Jeffrey grinned and punched me in the shoulder. "Say, can I take her lead?"

We walked a few paces in silence, LR trotting happily at my cousin's side. Then Jeffrey said, "You know, it wouldn't kill you to smile every once in a while, Bertie."

We didn't see any American generals. But as far as LR was concerned, we met someone even more exciting.

As we were walking near the main American military headquarters on the north side of the square, Jeffrey stopped short. A man in an American uniform was striding toward us. Or rather, the man was being hauled along by a feisty little black Scottish terrier. The dog scurried right over to sniff LR, who barked a greeting and wagged her stubby tail.

"You'll have to excuse Telek. He's such a flirt," said the American officer, with a friendly grin.

"She doesn't usually like other dogs," I told him.

"Of course she likes this one," said Jeffrey. "We were just saying that she's a good judge of character. He's the famous Telek, isn't he?"

"Oh, yes, and he's as popular as his master, General Dwight D. 'Ike' Eisenhower," the man chuckled.

"Telek is the supreme commander's dog," Jeffrey explained to me. "I read about him in the newspaper."

"Oh, yes, Telek is quite famous and goes with the general everywhere. Most recently, he's been with us for the Allied campaigns in North Africa and Italy. We even brought Telek to the States for a quick trip home before returning to London so General Eisenhower could take charge of the invasion. And that meant Telek had to be in quarantine here. But he's out now, much to the general's relief," the officer explained. "And who's this feisty lady?"

"Her name is Little Roo," I replied. "She's not a world traveler like Telek, but yesterday she helped rescue two children and their mum after a bomb hit their house."

"Is that so? Little Roo, I salute you," said the man. And he did just that. "You're doing more for the war effort than Telek here, who can't seem to tell the difference between rugs and grass. Still, he keeps the supreme commander happy." He nodded toward the large building at the north end of Grosvenor Square. "Well, we've had our walk. Now it's back to headquarters at number twenty. Have a nice afternoon."

As we watched them go, I asked Jeffrey, "How in the world did you know who he was?"

Jeffrey shrugged. "The American soldiers are always talking about Ike and his dog. I even know that the officer is Harry Butcher, his top aide. You could find out things too, if you came to visit. The soldiers don't mind having us around. They're friendly. I get chocolate bars every week." Jeffrey lowered his voice. "You'd be welcome. You know that."

I didn't answer. We walked along in silence for a few minutes. Jeffrey spoke again. "Bertie, you need to visit them. You can't keep avoiding your brother—or your mum."

"Did someone tell you to say that?" I could hardly trust my voice.

"No, but it's the truth. It's been too long. You can't keep hiding." He sighed. "It's not just about you, you know. You can't blame yourself. No one else does."

I shook my head. "That's not true."

"It *is* true, Bertie. Maybe it wasn't always, not at first. But it is now. And Will's much better. They're keeping him busy with physical therapy and everything, but he's got a tutor now and he's trying to catch up. We study together a lot."

I cut him off. "Let's go home." I grabbed LR's lead and stomped ahead.

It wasn't that I didn't love my brother. Or that I didn't miss Mum. But when I saw the scar on Will's face, or watched him limping, trying to be brave about his missing arm, all I could think was: *I did this. This is all my fault.* I couldn't tell Jeffrey that.

And I didn't see how Will or Mum could forgive me. I couldn't forgive myself.

CHAPTER FIFTEEN

- -

A cipher is a method of converting a message
into symbols . . . which have no meaning to a
person not possessing the key.

—*SOE Manual*

MONDAY

"Mr. Bradshaw, are you with us?" Mr. Turner's ruler
came down hard on his desk and I jumped in my seat.
"We're all waiting for your answer."

"I'm sorry, sir. Can you . . . can you repeat the question?" I glanced over at David, who was pretending to
yawn while frantically trying to mouth an answer to help
me out.

"What year was London founded and what was
its original name?" Mr. Turner repeated. "Surely you
learned this some years ago. But it was also in our reading this weekend."

I tried to gather my thoughts. David was holding up
five fingers. Five. "Oh, um, it was founded in AD 50 and
its name was . . . um . . ."

Mr. Turner cleared his throat, cutting me off. "Perhaps, Mr. Goodman, since you seem so eager to participate, you can help your friend out."

"The town was called Londinium, sir," David answered slowly. His cheeks were flushed. He really hated being singled out—or getting anyone else in trouble. "It was founded on the bank of the Thames about seven years after the Romans invaded England."

History was our last class of the day, and as we walked into the hallway, David touched my arm. "Sorry, Bertie. I only wanted to help you out. We should know better, I guess. Nothing gets by Mr. Turner."

"That's for sure. And I should've known that answer. I *do* know it. It's just . . ."

"Bertie, you've been acting strange all day."

"I'm just tired. There were two raids this weekend." As we walked down the hall, a boy jostled David's shoulder. Automatically, I glanced up to see who it was.

"It's fine, Bertie. He didn't do it on purpose," David said. "You don't have to fight my battles."

"I know." I bit my lip. David didn't like to talk about it. But I knew it still happened. A whispered word; an "accidental" elbow dig in the ribs.

It was always done in a sneaky way, always out of the sight of teachers, especially Mr. Turner, who'd made his position crystal clear on the first day. "There will be no bullying or anti-Semitic behavior of any sort in this class," he'd declared. "As Winston Churchill has said, we are waging war 'against a monstrous tyranny.' Our countrymen are dying for this cause. It is up to us to honor that sacrifice."

David had stopped to reach into his knapsack. He handed me a book. "Here, I brought that Sherlock Holmes story. Do you want to come to my house now and read it? I can show you what I know about ciphers."

"Not today. Sorry. I . . . I have to go to the command post." I stuffed the book into my knapsack, checking again to be sure the small red notebook was tucked safely at the bottom.

Straightening up, I caught sight of a worried look on my best friend's face. Besides Will, David was the bravest kid I knew. If I could tell him about Violette's notebook, I knew he'd want to help. I needed his help.

But I'd made a promise to Eleanor.

Eleanor was waiting for me outside the command post on Maddox Street. "Where's Little Roo? I thought you'd bring her. Is her paw all right?"

"She's fine," I said. "I came straight from school. I can't exactly take her there."

Eleanor's face fell. "Oh, I brought her an extra doughnut. But you can take it home with you."

Inside, Warden Hawk greeted us and I introduced Eleanor. "Uh, Warden Ita said we could use the meeting room this afternoon to do some homework."

"Fine with me," Warden Hawk said. "Glad to see

you're taking an interest in school again, Bertie. Now I'm headed out to join Warden Ita at a meeting about these new raids." He beckoned to a young woman who looked to be in her late teens. "Kids, this is Deputy Warden Esther. She's here to finish her training." He winked. "She wants to learn from the best."

Deputy Warden Esther laughed. "And, of course, the most modest."

Eleanor stepped forward to shake hands. "I'm so pleased to meet you. Will you be working in this post from now on?"

"No, I'll go back to the East End, where I live. It was hard hit in the Blitz, as you probably know. I want to do as much as I can for my community," Warden Esther said. "I was about to make tea. Would you like a cuppa?"

"Thank you," Eleanor and I replied together. I just hoped those "best" wardens hadn't told Warden Esther about my disastrous first raid on Friday night.

"What is it with you and shaking hands with everyone?" I mumbled after Warden Esther had brought us two steaming mugs and closed the meeting room door behind her. "You're worse than my cousin Jeffrey. He was here yesterday, showing off and chatting away all polite like to some American officer we met. The supreme commander's aide or something."

Eleanor bent down to reach into her knapsack. Her voice was muffled. "I guess I'm just used to being with adults. My father's taken me everywhere with him, though he didn't want to bring me here. I'm actually not really supposed to be in London, but I begged him not to send me to boarding school."

I fell silent. I wanted to ask about her mother, but I didn't want to pry. And I didn't want to answer any questions about *my* mum.

Eleanor placed a pencil case and a stack of paper on the table before her. She opened the pencil case, took out a pencil, and twirled it thoughtfully between her fingers. At last she spoke again.

"My parents have been divorced for a long time. I don't see my mother often. But since Nan—my father's mother—is from London, Father let me come with him. Even so, he lives in a separate part of Nan's home. It's like a little apartment. And I live with Nan in the other part."

"Why's that?"

"Something to do with security . . . because of Father's job in the war. I guess people who study literature are good at information analysis. That's why he got recruited."

"Analysis?"

Eleanor shrugged. "I think he tries to figure out what the Germans are doing and then hides *our* plans. It's very secret. Father says some of the men he works with at the OSS haven't even told their wives back in the States what they do."

Wives. In a flash, I remembered Saturday afternoon,

when the man had come out of the office on Baker Street and been startled to find his wife and big black dog standing there. His wife had seemed taken aback to see him too.

"Eleanor, do you remember Violette ever talking to your father about what he does in the war?" I asked.

"No, Violette barely spoke to Father, and he seemed as surprised as I was when she left so suddenly, though I suppose he could have been acting."

"Did she ever mention knowing a soldier, or someone who might have been involved in the resistance?" I asked.

"No. Violette did have a boyfriend, though. She called him Jay and said that he was very handsome and that they went dancing. But that's all." Eleanor took another pencil from her case and pushed it toward me. "She was a private person. Or maybe we weren't as good friends as I thought," she added. "Maybe she just thought of me as her young student."

Or maybe, I thought to myself, *Violette simply hadn't been allowed to say anything to anyone.* But Violette had violated the code of secrecy in one way—by keeping a notebook. And maybe some of the answers were in it.

Eleanor met my gaze. "I'm all ready. Do you have it?"

I nodded, reaching into my knapsack and placing the notebook between us. Eleanor stared at it for a moment, touching it with one finger, almost as if she didn't believe it was real.

I reached over and opened it. "These first pages are notes Violette took from her training lectures. She learned about surveillance and sabotage and living undercover. There's also a whole section about what to do with your parachute."

"Parachute? That's how people are sent to other countries?"

I nodded and found the page. Then I read aloud:

Today we learned about parachutes. After I land, I must hide the parachute. I can weigh it down with stones and drop it into a lake or river—or I can bury it. But I must do that at night. And try not to get muddy and dirty.

Our instructor even gave us the dimensions the hole should be, if a parachute must be buried: two feet long by two feet wide by two feet and six inches deep. I should cover it as naturally as possible with leaves and sticks. It's important to remember to clean my shoes afterward. He didn't say what to do with the spade. I'll ask about that tomorrow.

Eleanor let out a big breath. "I can hardly believe it. It's hard to imagine Violette jumping out of the sky. She's so elegant. She loved to tell Nan and me stories about getting all dressed up to go dancing. Nan said I should be more like Violette, since half the time my hair is snarly and I've got mud on my dress. Did she really parachute into France, Bertie?"

"Yes, I think she did." I flipped through to the last section. "Maybe that's when she started to use a secret code—once she was there, working for the French resistance."

"Let's start right in," Eleanor said, peering at the confusing string of letters. "Actually, I think technically this is called a cipher. I asked my father last night, and he said that even though people sometimes use the words *code* and *cipher* to refer to the same thing, there's actually a difference between the two."

"What do you mean?"

Eleanor settled on a page and pointed. "Well, see these letters? They're jumbled and don't make sense. You can tell right away they contain a secret message. That means this is a cipher. If it's a substitution cipher, one letter is substituted for another to make a new alphabet. There are other kinds too."

"How is a code different?"

Eleanor bit the end of her pencil. "Father admitted he isn't a real expert. But he did say that with a code, the words and letters make sense on the surface. But they have a hidden meaning you can't figure out unless you have the key to unlock the code."

I frowned. "I'm not sure I get it."

"Well, suppose you and I have an agreement that every time we write, *The dog is lost*, what we really mean is: *I'm in danger*. Or if I wrote you a note that said, *Let's read some Sherlock Holmes at the library*, you and I would have decided in advance that what that *really* means is: *Let's meet at the command post to work on the notebook.*"

"So, in that case, *Sherlock Holmes* stands for the notebook and *library* stands for the command post?"

"Exactly. But we can see that's not what Violette did here. These strings of letters don't make real words. So Violette was using some sort of cipher system."

"How do we figure out how to read her cipher alphabet?" I asked.

Eleanor shrugged. "That's about as much as I know, Bertie. Maybe we just guess."

"Seems like this could take a long time. And we have just a few days." I thought of David. If David was here, he'd probably have some ideas.

"We have to at least try," Eleanor said. She opened the notebook to the first page of code. "Let's start here."

We hunched over the letters. I wasn't even sure how to start. I could see Eleanor making scribbles. "Got it?"

"No!" she said. "Shh. Stop talking and concentrate."

We were silent for a while. I tried to make sense of the random letters. Nothing worked.

"I wish there were spaces between some of the letters, like with real words," I complained. "Nothing I try seems to work."

"There's got to be a better way to go about this," Eleanor agreed, tossing her pencil down. "We're wasting time. This could take us weeks!"

"I might have an idea," I suggested. I pulled David's book from my knapsack.

Eleanor read the title aloud. "*The Return of Sherlock Holmes*. What's that got to do with this?"

"My friend David gave me this book. There's a story in it about ciphers, but . . . but that's not the whole point." I took a breath. "What I'm trying to say is that I think we should ask David to join us. He likes reading about codes and ciphers, and he's a big fan of Sherlock Holmes. He might have some ideas about how to go about it."

"But . . . but that means telling someone else about Violette," said Eleanor uncertainly.

"I know. But if we want to solve this by Thursday, then . . ."

"All right. But he has to keep everything about this secret." Eleanor paused. "Do you trust him?"

"Yes, I trust him," I told her. "David's my friend, and that's what friends do."

PART THREE

Violette

To the question why people with so little
training were sent to do such important work,
the only reply is: the work had to be done,
and there was no one else to send.

—Rita Kramer, SOE historian

CHAPTER SIXTEEN

You should always be on the alert to notice
strangers hanging about, especially when you
are leaving any house.

—SOE Manual

TUESDAY

"Eleanor, this is David." We stood outside the Heywood Hill bookshop on Curzon Street. Eleanor and I had agreed to meet there since we couldn't use the command post that afternoon.

Eleanor, as expected, reached out to shake David's hand. "Bertie says you're a Holmes expert and you know about ciphers and he's your friend. So I trust you."

"Uh . . . uh, thanks," David mumbled, ducking his head a little so that a lock of shiny dark hair fell over his eyes. He brushed it aside. "Nice to meet you too. I haven't met many Americans before. But I like to read Edgar Allan Poe stories."

An elderly man with a cane was coming out of the

bookshop, followed by a younger woman. David was closest and sprang forward to open the door. "Watch your step, sir."

Suddenly I recognized the man. "Oh, you own the clock shop on Brook Street! I love looking at the antique watches in your window."

"With a name like Humphrey, it seemed like fate that I should open it, don't you think?" The old man grinned.

I had no idea what he meant but tried to smile politely anyhow.

"My daughter here keeps pestering me to retire, but I'm stubborn," he went on. "And I like to work."

"My foster grandfather does too," David put in softly. "He left Russia because of . . . because of the pogroms. He started a shoe shop on Berwick Street and still goes in almost every day."

David had told me he felt lucky to be living with the Rosen family. Some of the children who left Germany on trains like David did had been sent to stay in boarding schools or with Christian families. That made it hard to practice their Jewish faith.

"I imagine you help in the shop a lot," said Mr. Humphrey solemnly. He glanced at me and lifted his cane to point at my civil defense badge. "And I see you're a volunteer."

At least today I'd remembered to wear it. I needed to report to the command post for an early evening shift.

I even had my helmet and torch in my school knapsack. "I'm an air-raid messenger for the civil defense." I gestured toward Eleanor. "And Eleanor here is from America. She volunteers for the PDSA—the People's Dispensary for Sick Animals."

"Now, did you hear that, Lydia?" The man turned to the young woman behind him and chuckled. "America is sending us young girls to help protect the nation. I, for one, shall sleep much more soundly tonight."

"I also know your shop, sir," Eleanor piped up. "And I can guess why you named it Master Humphrey's Clock Shop."

Of course, Eleanor *would* know.

"Charles Dickens wrote and published a journal called *Master Humphrey's Clock*. My father and I were walking by once and he told me," she said. "He's here working for the war now but at home he teaches British literature."

Mr. Humphrey chortled with laughter. "What would we do without the Americans? They love our English authors as much as we do. And now we *really* can't do without the Americans." He leaned forward, adding in a conspiratorial whisper, "With Eisenhower at the helm, the invasion of France is just a matter of time. When and where will it be? That's what *everyone* wants to know."

Warden Hawk had said much the same thing, I remembered. And so had George and Jeffrey. Violette had written about the need for secrecy. Everything seemed to depend on it. And now, somehow, we were caught up in it too.

"Yes, the invasion is coming," Mr. Humphrey declared as he moved away. "And I intend to stand my ground long enough to witness it."

As we stepped into the warmth of the cozy bookstore, I mulled over Mr. Humphrey's words. David and I waited while Eleanor asked the clerk if we could do homework upstairs for an hour if we promised to talk quietly.

"I can't imagine the clerk will say no. Eleanor seems a very . . . determined sort of person," David whispered. I grinned and nodded.

Eleanor came over and beckoned us up the stairs. We followed behind her bouncing knapsack. "She said yes, as long as we move if we're in someone's way. It's not a big space."

Halfway up, Eleanor turned around, her eyes sparkling with excitement. In a low voice, she said, "And did you happen to notice who I was talking to? That clerk is Nancy Mitford."

David and I exchanged a glance. I whispered, "Uh, who's Nancy Mitford?"

"Oh, she's one of the glamorous Mitford sisters. She's been presented at the royal court. And best of all, she's a real novelist." Eleanor sprinted up the steps two at a time.

"I wonder if *all* American girls are like her," David murmured.

I shook my head. "I don't think anyone is quite like Eleanor."

"Are you two talking about me?" Eleanor gazed down at us from the top. "Come on, don't dawdle. We have work to do."

We settled on the floor in a corner. Eleanor shrugged off her coat and drew in a deep breath, as if she was inhaling the scent of roses. "Maybe it's because of my father, but I do love bookstores and books and stories. I think when I grow up, I might work for a newspaper."

"As a crime reporter?" asked David. "I wouldn't mind that. I like anything that has to do with detectives."

"Maybe. Have you ever heard of Nellie Bly? She's dead now, but she was a famous American reporter. She went undercover like a detective." Eleanor reached into her knapsack for her supplies. "I read that once Nellie pretended to be a patient in an asylum, to expose horrible conditions. I'd like to investigate like that. Or maybe travel to faraway places and become a war correspondent like Ernie Pyle."

"A war correspondent," David repeated thoughtfully. "Do you think *this* war will still be going on five or six years from now, when we're old enough to have real jobs?"

I shook my head. "It won't. We're going to defeat

the Nazis. My cousin Jeffrey says there are thousands of soldiers training in the countryside."

Eleanor set out paper and handed each of us a pencil. "Sometimes I wonder if humans will ever stop fighting wars. Nan has told me about World War I. So many men died, some people called it the war to end all wars. But it wasn't so long ago, was it? And now . . ."

"I can hardly remember when we didn't have rations and blackout curtains and bombs," I chimed in. The war was like London's cold, thick, wet fog. It seeped into you, through your clothes and into your skin and all the way inside, until the chill reached your heart.

"I was eight in January of 1939 when I came to London," David added in a low voice. "That was eight months before war was officially declared. But it had already started, at least for us and other Jewish families."

Eleanor reached out and touched his arm gently. "I'm so sorry."

For a minute, we were all silent. I was thinking about how the war was so big, like a giant wave crashing on a beach. And how we were all like tiny grains of sand, being tumbled around or swept away. A bomb from far away had somehow hit our house and almost killed my brother. David had been torn from his family. Eleanor had come to live in a new country.

And Violette. Violette had decided to dive into the path of the wave.

So I took out the small red notebook and put it in the center of our circle. "Maybe we should begin."

Eleanor looked at David. "Has Bertie told you about Violette and . . . everything?"

"Yes, he explained on our way here," David replied. "And I think trying to break the cipher is the right thing to do. Especially since she set the trap for this week—whatever it is. If something *has* happened to her, then maybe the answers are in here."

I just hope we can find them in time, I thought.

"You should look at it, David." Eleanor picked up the notebook and handed it to him.

We were quiet as David turned the pages. "It definitely seems like a cipher. She's made it harder to decode since there aren't any spaces to show where words begin and end, like in a regular sentence. That would make it easier to look for patterns, or small words that get repeated a lot. Words like *a* or *the* or *I*."

"Can we solve it?" Eleanor wanted to know.

"We can definitely try some things. But we might need to get help from a *real* expert, especially if we get stumped," David said. "And I have an idea who we can ask. My foster family knows Benjamin Marks, who owns a bookstore. Once, after Shabbat, we were chatting with him and my foster father told Mr. Marks how much I love detective stories." David lowered his voice. "Mr. Marks told us that his son, Leo, began learning about codes when he was a boy. He sort of winked and said,

'He's very good. And these days we tell everyone he's working for the Ministry of Labour.'"

"Oh, wow. That's his cover, I bet," I said. "We could visit the bookstore and ask to meet Leo. What do you think, Eleanor?"

Eleanor cocked her head. "Maybe. But let's see how far we get. And Violette might still come see me or claim the notebook before Thursday."

"And what about asking your father for help, Eleanor?"

"No, not yet," said Eleanor. "And it's not just that Violette trusted me with the notebook. I'm not sure he'd take me seriously. Father already thinks I spend too much time reading Nancy Drew mysteries."

"I wonder why Violette didn't go directly to your father for help," David mused.

"Maybe something happened to make her hesitate," I suggested, glancing at Eleanor.

"You mean she might be suspicious of people on her own side?" David raised his eyebrows.

"It's possible—you never know," I told them. I couldn't help remembering George's words and added, "There might even be traitors or double agents right here in London."

David scoffed. "Bertie, this is England! That doesn't seem very likely."

"You're probably right, David," said Eleanor slowly. "But the thing is, we can't be sure, not until we decipher all the entries in her notebook. And maybe not until Violette contacts me again. Or we find out what happened to her."

David shot me a doubtful glance. It was clear he thought Eleanor was imagining things. I said nothing. I didn't want to bring up the other possibility that had jumped to mind: that Violette herself had become a traitor and had started working for the Germans. And that maybe there was something hidden in the cipher that shouldn't be there.

"All right, then." David turned back to the notebook. "Maybe instead of trial and error, we should do some analysis first."

"Analysis? What do you mean?" I asked.

"We need to step back and put ourselves in Violette's shoes. We should examine what sort of person she is. That might give us a clue to the cipher system she decided to use," David explained.

"That makes sense." I turned to Eleanor. "You know her. Is she very precise?"

Eleanor twirled her pencil and stared at it. "She isn't messy—at least not about the way she looks. But she's not too picky either. She never made me redo my work to make it neater. I'd say she's in the middle."

"I have another idea," I said. "I've read more of the notebook than either of you." I picked it up and started paging through it. "Most of it is notes on what she was learning. I got so caught up in that section, I haven't read much more, but . . ." I found the page I wanted. "Look here! These pages are her last entries in plain English, before she starts writing in code. Maybe there's something here that will help us figure out her cipher."

"Let me read it aloud," Eleanor said. I handed her the notebook. She took a deep breath and began.

CHAPTER SEVENTEEN

At the last minute, I slipped this diary into my pocket. I know I shouldn't bring it. I should never have begun it in the first place. But I want to remember everything that is happening. Someday, perhaps, the world will be different and I can share it with my children, and with my young friend Eleanor. She dreams of her own adventures, I know.

"She did think of you as her friend, Eleanor," I said. Eleanor nodded, her face flushed with pleasure. "Oh, listen. Violette mentions my father in this next part."

When I first approached Dr. Shea about how I might volunteer, he made it clear I shouldn't say anything to Eleanor. And then, when he slipped me a piece of paper with a single name on it, he warned me not to tell even him anything more. I never spoke about my interviews. I'm sure he guessed, but I never explained why I couldn't tutor anymore.

I expect it's not easy for Dr. Shea to raise a daughter like Eleanor. She sees more than you realize. That's another reason I left without saying goodbye. I worried she would see through any lie I might have spun.

And now the moment has come. I am at the airfield, waiting for darkness. All my training has led me here. After tonight, I will write only in cipher. I'll keep this tiny notebook hidden. If I'm ever in danger of being caught, I'll burn it.

Socks, hat, dress, coat. Getting the right clothes to live in occupied France turned out to be much harder than I imagined. I even tore out the English labels from my underwear. Luckily, I still have a coat and hat I bought in Paris before the war.

Shoes were the worst! English shoes give you away. We learned that a German could be walking behind you on the street and find you out just by looking at your shoes. It took a while, but I finally found a pair that will do.

I've memorized my cover story too. I'm actually quite delighted with it. It's so unlike me! I'll pose as someone working for a company that sells patterns for baby clothes and blouses and dresses for ladies. I'll go door to door, calling on farmwives in the countryside and women in towns and cities.

"I hope I don't have to do any sewing demonstrations!" I joked when I got briefed about my cover. I love nice clothes, but I haven't ever been good at making them myself. I was given a sample booklet illustrating the garments, and even a few printed patterns in French. If I get stopped by Germans, I'll have something real to show them.

It makes sense in another way too. Women are especially suited for SOE work because most young men serve as soldiers or work in war munitions factories. German officers are more likely to be suspicious of a young man walking about in the middle of the day.

My cover will hide my true work as a messenger for Maurice (not his real name, of course). Maurice is the head of our Maquis—the local French resistance network.

"Maurice is a wily character. He's an old hand at this business. You can trust him," my instructor said. "Up to a point, that is."

"Why wouldn't I trust him?" I asked, alarmed.

"You should always be on your guard," he explained. "There may well be informers in the village. We've heard of resistance networks being infiltrated by enemy agents. And people can change sides."

"Can you be trusted?" I asked, half teasing.

He scowled. "Just be careful."

Maurice has found me a host family. Neighbors and friends will be told I'm a distant relative trying to earn money to attend university someday. I have a cover name: Marie Billard. I'll have to get used to being called Marie. I have a code name too, of course. But I won't write it here.

My duties will include making weekly reports to London on our sabotage activities and on German troop movements in the area. I'll code my reports myself, then bring them to Philippe, our radio operator.

In training, we learned various types of codes and ciphers. We were also given pre-arranged key phrases to use in telegrams or personal notices in newspapers. For instance, an agent might send a telegram saying: "Looking forward to seeing you at the wedding." What that might really mean is: "The operation is proceeding as planned."

The best sort of personal advertisement to put in a newspaper is one saying something has been lost. Otherwise, if you print a notice about, say, a bicycle for sale at a certain address, you might have people showing up to actually buy it!

My eight weeks of training are over. It was harder than I imagined, especially the parts on how to use dynamite and explosives. But the most terrifying thing of all was practicing the parachute jump.

And yet, somehow, I did it. I feel ready. Tonight—or after midnight on the morrow—under a full, bright moon, I'll drop into a field somewhere in France.

Eleanor paused and looked at us, her eyes wide. "There's no doubt, is there? Violette parachuted into France."

"And at night too," I said.

"Did you pay attention to what she said about codes?" David whispered. "I didn't realize spies placed hidden messages into notices in newspapers."

Eleanor was examining the notebook. "There's a little more in regular English. It's scribbled in pencil."

"Maybe she wrote it on the airplane," I guessed. "They might not have let her bring an English-made pen with her. It sounds like any tiny, small thing could give an agent away."

"Keep going, Eleanor," David urged.

And she did.

I'm on the noisy, cold, smelly plane. It's just me, alone in the back behind the pilots. So I can jot down a few more sentences.

I received last-minute instructions at the airfield. First, to my surprise, the boss came over to shake my hand and wish me good luck. "We have confidence in you."

Next, the code master walked me to the steps of the plane. "Be careful," he told me. "Sometimes agents get rushed and sloppy with their coding. Follow every step, and don't forget your personal security check. We've had to remind agents to do that in the past." The security check is a few extra letters of special code that are unique to each agent.

I promised. "Remember, I did well on my coding, better than on parachute-jumping practice."

We've been in the air for an hour now. The English

Channel looks silvery in the moonlight. But I know the seas are much rougher than they look from here. And sometime—sometime soon, perhaps—hundreds of ships carrying soldiers will journey across these waters to liberate all of Europe from Hitler's grasp.

The moon is playing peekaboo with rolling clouds. I hope the pilots can find the right field. I repeat the instructions to myself. "There are two ponds on this farmer's land. I should look down, situate myself, and pull at the parachute strings if I'm too close to the water."

Beside me sit two bags, with my clothes and supplies. One of the pilots will drop them out after me. There are explosives too. And I'm carrying a lot of French money. It'll be used for bribes and to help members of the Maquis with food and lodging costs.

Out the window, the clouds are dissipating into thin wisps. Soon we'll be over land, where the rivers will shine like silver ribbons in the dark landscape.

It's time.

CHAPTER EIGHTEEN

Good cryptographists are rare indeed.
                                    —Edgar Allan Poe,
                        "A Few Words on Secret Writing," 1841

When Eleanor finished, no one said anything for a long while. At last I cleared my throat. "Hearing it out loud like that makes her seem so real." As real as the young woman I'd found lying alone in the cold.

"She took such a risk," said Eleanor. "From one day to the next, she couldn't know who might be watching her; she couldn't tell a friend from an informer."

"I think it's brave to live undercover in that way, always in fear," David agreed. "I keep thinking of my parents back in Germany." He explained to Eleanor, "They sent me here for safety. But they couldn't escape, not in time. Horrible things were happening in Germany. One night in November of 1938, thousands of Jewish businesses were burned and destroyed. That was Kristallnacht—the Night of Broken Glass. Many Jewish people were arrested or sent away. Others were killed."

"You must have been frightened," Eleanor said.

"Yes, I wasn't even eight. Our train was full of children, some only two or three years old."

"Did you understand why you were coming to England?" Eleanor asked.

"Not really. I knew my parents were worried. Also, I'd already been forced to leave school because they'd made a rule that Jewish children weren't allowed. Papa said he and Mama would join me later. But they couldn't, especially after war was declared that September." David raised his thin shoulders in a slight shrug. "We don't know what's happening at home now. I don't get letters anymore."

We were all quiet for a long moment. I closed my eyes and felt a sharp pang of longing. I missed Mum. But at least I could see her again.

After a bit, David looked up. "Listen, maybe we should do more of that analysis now. Any ideas, Eleanor?"

"Well, what I just read reminds me of a diary," she began. "Violette wanted to keep an account for herself."

"And that might mean she didn't need to use a very complex cipher," I said. "So she could write fast. And because she didn't think anyone else would ever read it."

David's eyes brightened. "Hey, nice deduction, Bertie. Worthy of Sherlock. Maybe pinning down the time frame might help us. Eleanor, can you recall exactly when Violette stopped being your tutor?"

"It was right in the middle of May." Eleanor turned back a few pages. "Oh, and she writes that her training took eight weeks."

"I have an idea. I'll be right back." David jumped up and disappeared down the stairs.

While he was gone, Eleanor buried her head in the notebook. My mind raced with questions. It seemed as if Eleanor's father might have helped Violette become an agent—or at least take the first step. So why hadn't Violette contacted him when she returned to London? Did she really not trust him?

David reappeared, holding a 1943 calendar. "Your friend Miss Mitford was saving this old one to wrap parcels in." He flipped through the months. "Violette said the moon was full for her parachute drop. So if she started training in mid-May, that brings us all the way through June to mid-July. Let's see. It says here the full moon was on July seventeenth."

"What can we deduce from that?" Eleanor wondered.

"Well, it might help us guess what coding method she used," David explained. "Say that Violette arrived in France in July. Depending on how long it took her to escape back to England, she might have lived there until December. Maybe she wrote diary entries once a week, or monthly."

"Oh, I see!" Eleanor turned back to the encrypted section of the notebook. As she turned the pages, her lips moved as if she was counting. She looked up. "David, you might be onto something. The gibberish is divided into six separate sections. See, here she's drawn a line and begun again on a new page. And a little further on, she does the same."

"So we can make a hypothesis that she wrote once a month," I said. "Now what?"

We were silent for a while. David spoke first. "Do you keep a diary, Eleanor?"

She nodded. "I write in it at least once or twice a week."

"How do you start each entry?"

"Oh, I always begin with the date," she replied. "Do you think Violette's cipher system is based on dates?"

"It's worth a try," David said.

I opened the notebook to the beginning of the ciphertext. On a blank sheet, I copied the first few lines and held the paper up so we could all see.

```
w q o b h p s z w s j s w v o j s p s s b v s f s
t c f b s o f z m h k c k s s y g b c k h v s a c c b
k o g g c p f w u v h h v s b w u v h w z o b r s r
```

Eleanor picked up her pencil. "Father told me about substitution ciphers. Maybe she shifted her cipher alphabet so it started with the first letter of the month in which she was writing. So if she wrote this in July, the cipher alphabet would begin with *J*. Then you use the rest of the alphabet in order until you get to *Z*, and then you start over with *A*."

"That's called a Caesar cipher," David said. "Julius Caesar used shifts when he wrote to his generals." He shook his head. "I don't think she would've started with *J* for *July,* though."

"Why not?" Eleanor and I asked together.

"August comes next—and she couldn't start that entry's cipher alphabet with *A,* because then her words wouldn't be encrypted," David told us.

"Good point. I knew there was a reason I invited you," I teased. "Do you have another idea?"

"Well, there are lots of different ways to come up with a shift," David explained. "You can think of a significant number and then shift the alphabet that number of places. Maybe she used a shift of seven, say, since July is the seventh month. Then the first letter of her cipher alphabet would be *H.*"

"Let me try that," I said, looking at the letters again.

```
w q o b h p s z w s j s w v o j s p s s b v s f s
t c f b s o f z m h k c k s s y g b c k h v s a c c b
k o g g c p f w u v h h v s b w u v h w z o b r s r
```

I shook my head. "Well, if *H* is *A,* then *W* is *P.* That means this string would begin with *PJHUA.* Not a real word."

"Hmm," said David. "She could have based it on whatever day of the week she happened to be writing her entry, but then it would be totally random to us. We'd be back where we started: making wild guesses."

"Let's keep thinking about a possible system," I said. "What if she used the number of letters in the month's name to determine the shift? For instance, *July* has four letters, so if we shift four places, it's *B, C, D,* then *E.* So *E* would be the first letter of her cipher alphabet."

"Let me try it this time." Eleanor translated the first letters of the message. She frowned. "No, that doesn't work either. I get nothing that reads like real words."

"I still think her system might have something to do with dates. Maybe Violette devised a more complex Caesar cipher," David suggested. "She might have added two things together. For example, the shift could be the number of letters in the month's name *plus* the number of the month."

"I'm not following." I grimaced. "What do you mean?"

"Well, for July it would be four since the word *July* has four letters. Then she'd add seven, since it's the seventh month. So the shift would be—"

"Eleven. That would mean that the first letter would be . . . *L.* I'll check it," I offered. But I came to the same dead end. "*LFDQ.* Still gibberish! No, it's not that."

David sighed. "Maybe we do need to find an expert."

"Wait," cried Eleanor. "I have one more idea."

CHAPTER NINETEEN

The agent must not leave about, and, as far
as possible, must not carry, incriminating
documents, e.g. names, addresses, notes.

—*SOE Manual*

Eleanor scribbled furiously, biting her lip in fierce concentration.

"Eleanor, tell us," I begged.

"Shhh . . . wait. Just a second. I think this might—oh, I've got it!" Eleanor looked up in triumph. "It *is* a Caesar cipher. But Violette didn't use the English word for July. She used the French word, *juillet*, which is seven letters. And then she added seven to that, since it's the seventh month."

"Wow. Good work!" said David.

"Violette would be so proud of me for using my French." Eleanor beamed.

"So the first entry shifts fourteen spaces," I said. "And that means the alphabet begins with *O*."

I kept working on Violette's message with the shift

of fourteen letters, matching one letter, then the next. "Whew, this takes a while. But I have the first part. Ready?"

I held up the ciphertext:

```
w q o b h p s z w s j s w v o j s p s s b v s f s
t c f b s o f z m h k c k s s y g b c k h v s a c c b
k o g g c p f w u v h h v s b w u v h w z o b r s r
```

And then my translation:

```
i c a n t b e l i e v e i h a v e b e e n h e r e
f o r n e a r l y t w o w e e k s n o w t h e m o o n
w a s s o b r i g h t t h e n i g h t i l a n d e d
```

"It's still hard to read without the spaces between the words," Eleanor said.

"Let me write it out properly." In a minute, I had it:

```
I   can't   believe   I   have   been   here
for   nearly   two   weeks   now.   The   moon
was   so   bright   the   night   I   landed.
```

"Let's keep going," said David. "If we put the notebook in the middle and each work on a different paragraph, we'll get the first entry decoded more quickly."

A little while later, we were done. Eleanor took scissors from her case and cut out our finished paragraphs, then taped them in order onto a larger sheet of paper.

"You really are always prepared, aren't you?" I teased. "Go on, read it."

Eleanor cleared her throat and began.

I can't believe I have been here for nearly two weeks now. The moon was so bright the night I landed.

There is much to write about. But I must give an account of the night I arrived. I thought the drop would be easy. It wasn't. Things didn't go as planned. I guess they never do.

Clouds played hide-and-seek with the big round moon. At least it was clear enough for the pilots to find the field. I jumped. Yet even as I was drifting through the darkness, clouds billowed up above me in great clumps.

The ground was soft and damp; to my relief, the landing was easy. I leaped to my feet. I was gathering the folds of the parachute when I felt the first raindrops. There was a sudden, fierce shower. Someone was supposed to meet me. I was supposed to listen for a low whistle. The rain and gusty winds made that impossible.

Once I realized I was alone, I hid behind a tall, thick hedgerow crammed with bushes and rocks. I was too busy to be afraid. I tied some rocks into the parachute, trudged over to one of the ponds, and dropped it in.

I rubbed my hands together. "Au revoir, parachute!" For some reason, I giggled. I was nervous. Yet it felt good to be home on French soil again.

It's funny—I'd worried I might forget my training. But I could almost hear my instructor's voice in my ears. "Remember, it's dangerous for the farmers. After all, we're dropping British agents, explosives for sabotage, and forbidden radio sets on their land," he'd explained. "If a suspicious German patrol goes snooping around and finds a half-buried parachute, or one that has floated to the surface of a lake, that could mean arrest."

Knowing that I could cause trouble for someone else made me extra careful. Once the shower blew over, the moon peeked out again. I scoured the marshy fields for the two bags that had been dropped with me. I finally found them in a bog. What a close call! All my clothes, plus the sewing patterns and order books I needed for a convincing cover story, had almost ended up at the bottom of a pond.

I was especially relieved since I knew one bag contained a shipment of guns, each layered with thick grease for protection, along with a waterproof canister containing ammunition. These were for members of the Maquis to arm themselves with when taking on sabotage missions at factories, railroad tracks, bridges, or supply warehouses.

I dragged the bags across the field and hid them in the thick bushes of the hedgerow. I felt exhausted. By now, I was covered in mud. The rain had stopped, but I still saw no sign of anyone else.

It was almost dawn when I decided it would be safer to bury the bags and take just one small suitcase with me. I took out what I needed and began to dig. Luckily, I'd been provided with a short-handled spade. I couldn't have done it using rocks or my bare hands.

Finally I was ready. I had directions to the farmhouse

where I'd be staying. The spade presented a dilemma. At first I didn't want to throw it in the pond. How would I dig up the bags later? Then I reasoned that once I made contact, I'd meet resistance members who had access to tools. So I tossed the spade in the water and washed off my hands.

I slipped behind the hedgerow, changed my mud-splattered trousers for a simple brown skirt and jacket, and twirled my hair into a neat bun. All the while, I listened for the sound of vehicles.

The extra money was also worrisome. I stuffed it into my underwear. It would be found if I was caught and searched. But, well, I would have to be caught first. I didn't intend for that to happen.

I glanced down at my feet. I'd almost forgotten. Too much mud! I remembered the warning that any small thing could give me away. I took off my shoes, tiptoed back to the pond, rinsed the outsides off well, and put them back on.

When it was nearly light, I heard a low whistle. My escort had been delayed, but he hadn't been detected. I showed him where the bags were buried. He assured me the Maquis would fetch them and deliver the rest of my things to me when it was safe.

What a long night! But I made it.

My host family is kind. The husband and wife pretend I am Marie, a hardworking girl. They don't ask questions. It's safer that way.

I love being able to speak French again. And I'm ready to start my new life as a pattern saleswoman. But I can't forget my true purpose.

I'm here for the cause of freedom.

CHAPTER TWENTY

Never relax your precautions, and never fool
yourself by thinking that the enemy are
asleep. They may be watching you all the
time.

—*SOE Manual*

That evening, I opened the door to Trenchard House.
The first thing I heard was a squeal. Then a horrible
thud. Next came a sharp yelp, and a man's low, angry
mutter. "Serves you right. You're a darn nuisance."

The door slammed behind me. I bolted down the
corridor. At the reception desk, I stopped in my tracks.
"Jimmy?" I stared, my mouth open. "Did . . . did you
just kick my dog?"

"Calm down, Bertie. I barely touched her with my
boot. She got out of your flat," he replied, putting his
hands up as if to hold me off. "There's a reason they
killed dogs when the war started, you know. There isn't
enough food for them. You should be home after school
to take care of your dog, not out gallivanting with your
girlfriend until dark."

"I wasn't!" I cried, bending down to gather the furry bundle in my arms. LR whined and pushed her muzzle into my neck. I could feel her shaking all over and I tightened my grip.

"Well, she's been after my biscuits, and I've got work to do. So take her away, will you?"

I opened my mouth to say more, but no words came out.

"Go on, Bertie. Don't just stand there."

I backed away and I could feel my face turning red. I wasn't strong enough to stand up for my dog.

The flat was still and cold. I tiptoed into the kitchen and put LR down gently. I felt hungry and tired. I hung up my old jacket and dropped my knapsack to the floor with a clunk. My bag was heavy. In addition to my helmet, I had my history book. I wasn't sure I could keep my eyes open long enough to concentrate. I sighed. I wasn't looking forward to more of Mr. Turner's questions.

"I'm sorry, girl. That wouldn't have happened if we'd been in our old house," I whispered. "I hate this place, LR. It's not home. We shouldn't be living here."

But we were.

Dad had left me a plate of cold macaroni and cheese, and a note in scratchy handwriting. He had a double shift starting early in the morning, so he'd turned in already. There was a P.S.: *Bertie, glad to see you remembered your helmet.* Dad was trying. We were both trying.

Most likely, Dad had taken LR out to the courtyard before turning in. He'd probably forgotten to close the flat door firmly when they came back in. It was no surprise that Little Roo had wandered out to the reception desk. The smell of food—even the crackling of a biscuit wrapper—could set her off. She'd recently figured out that the whistle of a teakettle went along with a meal. Or at least a bite of toast for her.

I grabbed a small saucer and put half of my macaroni and cheese into it. "Here you go, LR. I'm sorry you got so hungry, little one."

I picked up my fork and stabbed a piece of macaroni. I pushed it around and around on my plate, trying to make a bit of cold cheese stick to it. A clock on the wall ticked into the silence. In our old kitchen, it had never been quiet enough to hear a clock.

I could still see it in my mind, like a painting or even a movie with sound and action. In the summer, an old jar filled with daisies sat on the table. Mum would be taking scones out of the oven. I could almost taste them. They dripped with sweet cream butter and homemade red raspberry jam from our grandmother's bushes in the country.

"I'd better put some aside for your father or you two will devour them all," Mum would tell Will and me, laughing.

I had a hard time going to sleep. I kept thinking about something Violette had written in her notebook: The agent is surrounded by enemies, seen and unseen.

I'd never seriously imagined Jimmy as an enemy

before. I mean, I knew Jeffrey didn't like him. He'd seemed to sense something dark lurking behind Jimmy's cheery exterior. And if he had kicked her before, that would explain why LR shied away from him.

But could it be more than that? Both George *and* Jimmy had been there on Friday night when Violette had disappeared. Could Jimmy somehow be involved in this mystery?

Jimmy had gotten to Mill Street just before Warden Hawk and I had. But I'd never asked: Had the two constables come together from Trenchard House? Was it possible that one of them—or both—had already been lurking near Mill Street?

Violette had told Eleanor she had a boyfriend named Jay. What if Jay wasn't the name Jay, but simply the letter *J*, short for James or Jimmy? Jimmy Wilson.

Sinking down, I pulled the covers over my head and tried to make my mind stop spinning. Jimmy might not be the nice person I'd thought he was. And George might be bitter about what had happened to him. That didn't make either of them German agents.

I'd always let my imagination run wild. When I was little, I'd even thought Sherlock Holmes was a real, living person, not just a character in fiction.

I looked over at the empty bed. I'd always relied on Will to show me the way.

CHAPTER TWENTY-ONE

The introduction of an agreed name, word or
phrase into the text . . . will give the pre-
arranged message. e.g. The name "John" might
mean—"I am going into hiding immediately."

—SOE Manual

WEDNESDAY

I stopped home after school to fetch LR. I didn't want
to take the chance she'd get out again, like last night.
David went straight to the command post to meet Eleanor. I wondered what story she would spin to explain his
presence to the wardens. I didn't put it past her to claim
I needed help from both of them.

"Sorry to be late. My dad has a double shift today,"
I explained, opening the door of the meeting room. "I
didn't want to leave LR alone for that long."

"Oh, you brought her. Hello, Little Roo!" Eleanor
exclaimed, leaping out of her chair. LR spun in circles,
jumped up to lick Eleanor's face, and then made a bee-
line for Eleanor's knapsack.

"She loves you, Eleanor, but she loves food more." David grinned. "I think it's a safe deduction that you have something to eat in there."

Eleanor pulled out half of a smashed sandwich. "I saved part of my lunch on purpose." She turned back to us and her expression changed. "Listen, yesterday we made a good start. But time is running out. If Violette set a trap for someone this week—"

"I know. Then it could be up to us to make sure it works," I finished.

"Yes, and that's why . . . why I stayed up late." Eleanor opened her knapsack and brought out some sheets, along with Violette's notebook, which she'd taken home last night.

David glanced at the pages. "Hey, you decoded more of her journal, didn't you?"

Eleanor grinned. "I only had time to decipher August. If we work on September, October, and November today, that will leave only one more: December."

"That last entry might hold the key to everything, but I don't think we should skip ahead," I said. "We might miss something else important."

"And did the Caesar cipher system work for August?" David wanted to know.

"*Mais oui.*" Eleanor chortled. "It certainly did. In French, August is *août*. That means the shift is twelve— eight for the eighth month, plus four for the number of letters in *août*."

"And so *A* is—" David put in.

I'd already been working on it. *"M,"* I finished for him.

"September, October, and November are *septembre, octobre,* and *novembre,*" Eleanor went on. "So the alphabet shifts eighteen letters for September, nine plus the ninth month; seventeen for October, seven plus ten; and nineteen for November, eight plus eleven."

"Whew! I wish we had a way to work on this at the same time," I said. "It would go a lot more quickly."

Eleanor flashed a mischievous grin. "Well, we do, actually. Last night I copied out three sections from the notebook onto separate sheets. I'll take September." She slid paper covered with ciphertext toward each of us as solemnly as Mr. Turner passed out his exam questions. "Here's October for you, David, and November for you, Bertie."

"Let's decode and then read them in order," I suggested. "Maybe we'll find some answers to why she came back." *And where she is now,* I thought to myself.

I was just starting to copy out the regular alphabet on one line, with my cipher alphabet below it, when David cleared his throat.

"Uh, I worked on something too," he said, reaching into his knapsack and drawing out some pieces of paper. "A cipher wheel. I read about it in a book once. I started it in history class."

I laughed. "So that's why you didn't know the answer

when Mr. Turner called on you. I wondered what you were doing."

"But what's a cipher wheel?" Eleanor asked.

"I'll show you how it's put together," David said. "A cipher wheel actually consists of two alphabet wheels, an outer one and an inner one. Here we have a wheel with the alphabet in order from *A* to *Z*. Like this."

He held up a piece of paper with the alphabet written in a circle.

"Now, that's as far as I got in class. But the rest is easy. Do you have a pair of scissors, Eleanor?" David asked. And, of course, she did. David cut out another circle, smaller than the first. He added the letters of the alphabet and placed the circle inside the outer wheel, with the two *A*s lined up.

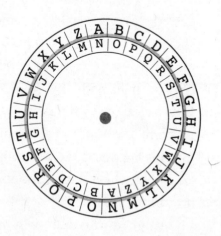

"It works like this. Say the shift is thirteen spaces. You just twist the inside wheel thirteen places," he explained. "*N* becomes the first letter of the cipher alphabet, and you can see the whole rest of the alphabet too."

"That's ingenious!" cried Eleanor. "Now we can twirl the inner wheel to easily see different cipher alphabets. Let me try." She moved the inside wheel. "So if the shift is seven, *H* is the beginning of the cipher alphabet and it looks like this."

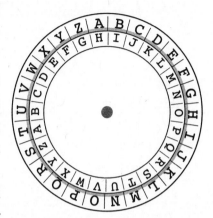

In a few minutes, we'd each made our own cipher wheel. I set mine for a shift of nineteen, for the month of *novembre*. "Got it. My cipher alphabet begins with *T*."

Little Roo had finished her sandwich and sat at Eleanor's feet, her stumpy tail vibrating against the floor. "There's no putting anything past you, is there, girl?" Eleanor reached into her knapsack again. "American Red Cross doughnuts. I brought one for each of us, including you, Roo."

LR *woof*ed and snatched it out of her fingers, then retreated to a corner. I took a bite of my doughnut and pulled the November section toward me. We worked in silence. When we were all finished, we passed our transcriptions to Eleanor.

"I don't have to be the one to read aloud all the time," she said.

"No, it sounds nice when you read," David said. "When I close my eyes, I can imagine Violette speaking."

"All right." Eleanor cleared her throat. "I'll begin where we left off, with August."

CHAPTER TWENTY-TWO

The Normandy countryside is lovely now. The August meadows are bright with wildflowers—pink, gold, and white. Lavender and honeysuckle perfume the soft air. Cows graze peacefully. Oh, how I love my native land. It's almost possible to forget that France is an occupied country.

Almost—but not quite.

There is a garrison of German troops in the village, a short bicycle ride from the farm where I'm staying. Madame and Monsieur P (I won't use their real names) have been gracious. They've told their neighbors I'm the daughter of a distant cousin, who is eager to earn money to go to university after the war. Whether everyone believes this story, I can't say.

My days are busy. Maurice has taken me to meet

a few members of this network. He is, in reality, an old friend of Monsieur P's, so it's natural that he should often visit the farm. That's when he gives me my assignments.

I've learned some surprising things during Maurice's visits. Although Maurice looks like an old peasant, he was an artist in Paris before the war began. It's a good reminder: I'm not the only one with a cover story.

Sometimes I travel by bicycle, other times by bus or train. I don't carry weapons, but messages: mostly information about factories or railroads that are targets for sabotage. Our network isn't large, but our members are brave.

I've taken part in a few operations myself. Last week I served as a lookout when we placed dynamite to damage a railroad bridge. The next day I rode by and saw train cars with artillery pieces stopped on the tracks. I smiled to myself. The Germans won't be able to deliver weapons to their defense bunkers on the coast until the bridge is repaired.

After that success, we radioed London to let them know about the stalled munitions, and to give the Allied air forces a chance to target the train. I hope none of the guns it carries will ever point toward the sea.

I feel that at last I'm doing something that matters: giving Allied troops a better chance of victory when the fateful day of the invasion arrives.

Philippe, who operates our wireless radio, lives in a small town about three miles away. His cover is working at a repair shop that fixes farm machinery, equipment, and household items like sewing machines. It's very convenient: The shop is a good place to exchange messages and coordinate arrangements.

Philippe has a gentle smile and a calm way about him. His French is excellent, but sometimes when we talk, I suspect he's not a native speaker. I've wondered if, like me, he came here from London.

We don't say any of this aloud, of course. We keep our meetings brief. Each week I code my report and bring it to him to send to London on his wireless set. I'm very careful and always remember to add my code name, BOOK, and to follow instructions for the extra security check, a string of letters to show I authorized the message. I haven't forgotten our code master's warning.

Eleanor stopped and placed the last page down. "That's August."

"So far, it seems to be going well for Violette," David noted. "But in the October entry I decoded, things start to become . . . more difficult."

I nodded, thinking of Violette's November entry. "Keep going, Eleanor."

She nodded and took a breath.

Things have been going well—up to now. But at the beginning of September, a new officer took charge of the garrison of German soldiers in the village. Maurice says the other man was lazy and liked to sit around and eat. His replacement seems eager to make his mark and crack down on any resistance activities.

Yesterday two German soldiers stopped me as I walked through town after visiting Philippe. They examined my papers and asked me questions. Everything was in order, but I felt nervous. This hasn't happened before.

Luckily, I wasn't carrying much money, as I often do. Perhaps I've gotten a little careless and should bring only the amount of money that matches my orders for sewing patterns. This might mean making more than one trip a week to see Philippe, though. That would add danger too.

I wondered if the soldiers followed me from the repair shop itself. I don't think so. But it's a reminder to be on guard at all times. Tonight I took this notebook out from under a floorboard in my little room. By the light of my candle, I read over all my notes on surveillance, just to refresh my memory.

It's been several weeks since I've written. It's October now, and so much has changed. Fear has begun to seep into my life like a thick London fog.

Maurice has shared some disturbing news about another resistance group in this region. SOE networks have code names too, by the way. Our network is SYCAMORE. The other network's code name is PINE. Maurice and the PINE leader sometimes meet secretly to share information.

Maurice learned that the PINE radio operator was captured by the Germans three weeks ago. Yet after that, the SOE office in London still sent two more agents by parachute to a field used by the PINE network. Both times, Germans were waiting on the ground to arrest the agent.

My heart raced when I heard this. Why had it happened? Our procedure is always the same: We are supposed to send an all-clear message the very day of a drop, to let the SOE in London know it's safe to proceed. But if the PINE radio operator had been captured three weeks ago, no all-clear messages could have been sent since then!

"London should have figured out that the PINE network has been exposed," I said. "No agent should be dropped without that go-ahead signal."

Maurice gave a small shrug. "Perhaps an all-clear message _was_ sent, and therefore London didn't realize the radio operator had been captured."

I let his words sink in. "You're saying that the Nazis seized the operator's radio and are pretending to be him. They're sending messages saying it's safe to drop more agents. But, Maurice, if the special security check is missing, then the SOE in London should be suspicious that something is wrong. The people there should figure out that the radio has been captured and the Nazis are impersonating the operator. They should know!"

Maurice's eyes were troubled. "Yes, London should be

able to figure out that the Nazis are either forcing him to send messages or, most likely, simply operating it themselves and conveying false information."

"The lack of the special security check should be a warning flag," I said again, shaking my head in disbelief. We'd been instructed what to do if we were ever captured and the Nazis forced us to transmit a radio message. The enemy might dictate the message and we'd be forced to send it. But we should leave off the special security check at the end.

"*Mais oui*, but sometimes radio operators get sloppy," Maurice said. "Even Philippe has forgotten his security check once or twice. It's easy to do when you're rushed."

"What happened when Philippe left it off?"

Maurice shook his head. "Ah, well, that's what worries me. When that happened, London simply sent back a message reminding him to be more careful."

I frowned. "That's not very reassuring—or professional."

At this, Maurice laughed. "Do you think it's professional to send young women like yourself into enemy territory with just a few weeks of training? We're all making this up as we go along—including the folks at the SOE London bureau. We're all flying by the seat of our pants." He was quiet for a while. "Of course, there is another possible explanation."

We were outside, standing near Madame P's kitchen garden, which still boasted autumn tomatoes, squash, pumpkins, and a few peppers. Stars sparkled above. All was peaceful and quiet, but Maurice's words made me shiver.

I lowered my voice. "You can't be suggesting what I think you are: that someone in London is <u>choosing</u> to ignore the lack of a security check. That someone there is complicit in what is happening. That we have a traitor."

"*Je ne sais pas.* I don't know. Not yet, anyway." Maurice gave a small shrug. In the light of a waning moon, the stubble on his chin looked like silver frost.

After he'd gone, I took out this notebook and reviewed my training notes. I can't afford to let down my guard or relax precautions. The enemy is watching at all times.

And if the Nazis have penetrated one network, ours might be next.

A few weeks have passed. It's now November, and something terrible has happened.

One morning last week, I went to the repair shop to deliver a message to Philippe. We were being cautious, but we needed supplies, and more help. So Maurice told me to give London the all-clear sign for an agent and explosives to be dropped that night. Philippe's radio message would let London know to proceed.

The moon was full. The plane would take off from England, just as mine had. After midnight, I was to meet the agent at the field and guide him or her to a designated safe farmhouse.

But when I bicycled in to let Philippe know, he wasn't at the repair shop.

"Is he sick?" I asked Jacques, the owner.

He shrugged. "Mademoiselle, I haven't seen him in four days."

Jacques is a thin older man with hard eyes that give nothing away. I felt a chill sweep over me. Was he an informer who'd discovered Philippe's true identity?

I had no way of knowing if the SOE in London would go ahead. But, recalling my own fear and sense of loneliness the night I'd arrived, I knew what I had to do. I decided to go to the field. If the agent was dropped, I'd remain hidden until I was sure it was safe.

I was very careful that day. I hid in a secluded hedgerow near the village for most of the afternoon. At dusk, I set out for the drop location, cutting across fields whenever I could. It was cold and my breath was frosty. I found a hiding place for my bicycle and myself in some thick brush. I waited, beating my arms to try to stay warm.

And then, at midnight, I heard the drone of the airplane. A single parachute swayed into the moonlit sky, followed by several large bags, probably full of explosives.

The night was still and quiet. I waited. Just as I was about to race across the field, I caught the sound of a rumbling car engine. From my hiding spot, I saw what happened next. The vehicle stopped on the road. Two figures emerged. They strode across the field, pointed guns, and shouted at the agent. A little while later, the car started up again. There were three people in it.

I waited, shivering, for another hour. Then I bicycled home in the darkness.

It is a few days later. I went back, once, to the repair shop. I looked through the window. No Philippe. I fear there can be no doubt: He's in the hands of the Nazis.

The London office might have made a mistake that compromised our network. But it could be something else. Maurice was afraid to put it into words. But it's possible that there's a traitor—a double agent—in the London bureau.

This possibility fills me with a deep, cold fear. If this situation continues, how many innocent agents might die? And as the invasion approaches, could this leak expose the date and location to the Nazis?

I stayed hidden in the farmhouse all week, hoping to hear from Maurice, fearing that if he'd been captured too, I was sure to be next.

And then tonight, just before dusk, Maurice appeared, looking worn and tired. It was chilly, but we went outside to talk in the orchard. A few bruised apples lay under the trees. I plucked two, only slightly worm-eaten, from a branch. We sat on a boulder to talk.

Maurice took a bite. He observed wryly, "I feel like this poor fruit: bruised and battered but not yet fallen."

"Where have you been?" I whispered. "I've been worried. . . ."

"I'm sorry. It couldn't be helped, Marie," he said, using my cover name.

"Have you found Philippe?" I asked.

He nodded. "The Nazis have him. By now he's on his way to one of their prison camps. But for a few days he was held in the German garrison in the village."

"Did you find a way to speak with him?"

He nodded. "We weren't able to break him out, but I was able to sneak into the garden long enough to have a whispered conversation through his cell window."

"What did you find out?"

"It's not good news. Philippe speaks German as well as French. But he never let his captors know he could understand them. So he was able to overhear a lot. Philippe says the Nazis are playing a sly game. Our worst fears are true: The Nazis have a high-level contact in our London bureau."

"A double agent," I whispered. "A traitor."

"Oui. And now the Germans are sending radio messages, purportedly from me, saying that both Philippe and you have been turned by the enemy."

"Turned? You mean they're saying we are working for the Germans? Why would they say that?"

"Ah, well. Obviously our traitor wants to cover for himself. He wants to be sure no one in the London office suspects him. My guess is he's a higher-up. When he says the radio operators aren't competent enough to include their security checks, people believe him.

"Also, if by any chance you or Philippe make it back to London, this means you'll be suspected of working for the Nazis. Most likely you'll be considered a risk and put into prison for the rest of the war—just in case the allegations are true."

"In other words, it's all part of the traitor's plan," I said. "It's a plot to undermine us."

Maurice nodded. "I'm afraid he's been getting away with this for some time. Somehow. Because I heard about something similar happening to two other agents who escaped to England. No one believed their story, and they've been put in Brixton Prison in London."

I felt like a heavy weight had fallen on me. "It's so horrible! One traitor in London is working with the Nazis to weaken the resistance. And his actions are sending innocent agents into the clutches of the Nazis."

"Yes, it's insidious. And most likely the Germans are sending false reports about everything. But someone in London is making sure the Nazis are in the loop, receiving information, explosives, and agents...." He paused.

"And any early alerts about the time and place for the invasion could land right in the hands of the enemy," I whispered. "But what can we do?"

"We have to abandon SYCAMORE. It's too dangerous to continue our work, at least for the time being," Maurice said. "I'm heading to Paris in the morning."

"Should I go with you?"

He shook his head. "No, I have another idea. It will be ... very dangerous, Marie. I'm not sure it will work."

He hesitated, but I'd already realized what I had to do. "I must get to London and try to stop this. Otherwise, more agents will die. The invasion itself could be at risk if details are leaked to the Germans." I looked Maurice straight in the eye. "But how? How can I find the traitor? It seems impossible."

For the first time, Maurice grinned. "Perhaps it is not as impossible as you imagine. Philippe did overhear some information that could help: the code name of the traitor. And I just happen to have an idea for how you might trap him—or *her*...."

He whispered the code name in my ear. And then we made a plan.

PART FOUR

The Truth

When you have eliminated the impossible,
whatever remains, however improbable,
must be the truth.

—Sherlock Holmes, in *The Sign of the Four*

CHAPTER TWENTY-THREE

I thought that I could be much more useful
in France, pushing the Germans out, than in
England doing paperwork. I applied to the
Inter-Services Research Bureau.

      —Pearl Witherington Cornioley, SOE agent

"That's it," Eleanor whispered. "November stops there."

"We *have* to decode this last part," said David. "It must have details about her plan."

I nodded, grabbing Violette's notebook. "It should be easy if she used the same system as before. And this last section is very short too. It's not even a page. What's December in French, Eleanor?"

"It's *décembre*."

"Eight letters. If we add twelve to that, since it's the twelfth month, we get a shift of twenty." I grabbed my cipher wheel and turned it. "That means the cipher alphabet starts with *U*."

Eleanor and David peered over my shoulder at the string of text that began the last part of Violette's journal:

bydtbnopuofgnqqnlfbyotbtdpfntandqby
dnqwflmodvltdenstphnndnxjfpniqsopopbylnjflq

I translated a few letters, using a shift of twenty. The first four letters were *H, E, J,* and *Z.* I shook my head. "This isn't going to work."

"Maybe she was on her journey here in December and couldn't write until January," David suggested.

"Good idea. January is *janvier* in French, Bertie," said Eleanor. "That would be a shift of seven plus one, since it's the first month of the year."

I tried a shift of eight, with a cipher alphabet beginning with the letter *I.* A minute later, I shook my head. "That's not it either."

We used our cipher wheels to test out various possibilities. We tried a shift of four, for the number of letters in Violette's last name, Romy. We tried beginning the cipher alphabet with the letter *L,* for *London.* We tried a shift of eighteen, adding up one plus nine plus four plus four, for the year, 1944.

We twirled the wheel again and again.

"Nothing. Nothing works!" I cried. "But we have to solve it. This message might include the code name of a traitor—and details of the trap she set for him."

A trap that is set for tomorrow night, I thought.

"I wonder if knowing more about her organization would help. It's not the same as the OSS, where Father works. Violette called it . . . let's see, the SOE." Eleanor scanned the transcribed pages. "And somewhere in the beginning I think she mentions something about Baker Street. But we would have no idea exactly where it is."

"Uh, um . . . actually we do," I told them.

"What?" Eleanor and David said together.

"I am pretty sure the SOE, the Special Operations Executive, is inside a building at 64 Baker Street. Even though the sign on the outside says something different: the Inter-Services Research Bureau."

"Hey, that's just down the road from 221B Baker Street," David said. He turned to Eleanor. "That's not a real place. It's the fictional home of Sherlock Holmes."

"Yes, and very early in her training, Violette finds out that a nickname for SOE agents is the Baker Street Irregulars, who were the kids Sherlock used to get information."

"Hold on a minute, Bertie," Eleanor put in. "Something doesn't make sense to me. On Saturday afternoon, I tracked you to a building on Baker Street. But Violette doesn't give an exact address in her notebook. Why . . . how did you know to go there?"

"Well, uh, it's like this. You were following me. But I was tailing someone else. Someone who might work there," I replied. "I don't know his name or what he does. I just call him Q—short for quarry."

"So why were you following him, Bertie?" David asked.

"Well, I first spotted him the night of the air raid. He

was running in the same direction as you, Eleanor. He might . . . he might even have been following you and Violette, though I can't say for sure."

"What? And you're just telling me now?" she cried, slamming her fist down on the table. "I don't believe this, Bertie. I thought we were a team."

"We . . . we are. And I was planning on telling you but . . . well, I didn't know how he fit into the mystery. I still don't. And I didn't want to scare you."

"Scare me? Most likely you just wanted to solve this mystery all by yourself." Eleanor began stuffing papers into her knapsack. "I can't believe you've been keeping this secret."

She started to get up but I reached out a hand. "Don't go, Eleanor. I'm sorry."

All at once, Eleanor sank down. She took in a deep breath. And then she whispered, "I have a confession. I've been keeping a secret too. Bertie, I told you that Violette asked me to keep the notebook until Friday and then she'd contact me, right?"

I nodded.

"Well, she had time to tell me a little more. Violette said if I didn't hear from her by Friday, then I should take the notebook to my father and ask him to get it to the highest American official in charge of the invasion that he could." Eleanor paused. "She said the notebook contained the truth. And if things didn't go as planned, we should try to get someone to believe it."

If things didn't go as planned.

David let out a low whistle. "All the more reason to figure this out now. It might contain evidence that Q is the one sending agents into the arms of Germans."

"Or it could be someone else," I said.

They both looked at me, wide-eyed.

"Not that I have any ideas," I added quickly. "I'm just saying that we still don't have all the facts. And it might reveal how she planned to trap him."

"But what can we do?" Eleanor asked. "Today is Wednesday and Violette said she'd set the trap for tomorrow night."

We were all quiet. My head spun with questions: Was Violette in hiding? Would she be able to follow through on springing the trap, whatever it was? Was she even alive?

I decided not to mention the wild ideas I'd had about Jimmy and George. They'd probably just been unfounded suspicions. But another possibility popped into my mind. If Jimmy had been Violette's boyfriend, maybe her disappearance was totally unrelated to her work as a secret agent.

I shook my head to clear it. I was getting off track. We needed to focus on decoding the rest of Violette's journal.

Eleanor bit her lip. Tears glistened in her eyes, but they didn't fall. "We don't have enough time! I don't see how we can do it."

David said quietly, "Sometimes people do the impossible. Remember, Bertie, what Mr. Turner told us about the Danish people rescuing their Jewish neighbors? And look at me, and the others who came here on trains. Thousands of us are here, and alive, only because a few people did what others thought couldn't be done."

David paused and took a breath. "Eleanor, all I'm saying is we can't give up. Not yet. We still have time before it gets dark. I think we need to get help from an expert. Let's try to find Leo Marks at his father's bookshop. We need to find out everything he knows about ciphers. And we don't have a moment to lose," he went on, stuffing papers into his knapsack. "It's like Sherlock rousing Watson and saying, 'Come, Watson, come! The game is afoot. Not a word! Into your clothes and come!'"

"Yes, let's go." Eleanor shot to her feet.

"You too, Little Roo!" I said.

Spy Practice Number Three

ATBASH CIPHER

```
blfix  levir  hgsvo  ruvds  rxsbl  flfgd
ziwob  ovzwr  mliwv  iglxl  mxvzo  gsviv
zokfi  klhvl  ublfi  kivhv  mxvzm  wgsvv
ckozm  zgrlm  dsrxs  blftr  evlub
lfikz  hgzmw  kivhv  mghlv  nzmfz  o
```

The Atbash cipher was originally developed to encode the Hebrew alphabet; it gets its name from Hebrew letters. However, it can be used with any alphabet.

This cipher works by reversing the alphabet, so that *A* becomes *Z*, *B* becomes *Y*, and so forth. Since it doesn't rely on a key or clues, it is very easy to break. For this reason, no hints are needed to decode this message. But it is also longer than the other practice messages. And while there are spaces between cipher letters, they do not represent actual word breaks.

PLAIN	A	B	C	D	E	F	G	H	I	J	K	L	M	N	O	P	Q	R	S	T	U	V	W	X	Y	Z
CIPHER	Z	Y	X	W	V	U	T	S	R	Q	P	O	N	M	L	K	J	I	H	G	F	E	D	C	B	A

CHAPTER TWENTY-FOUR

The world is full of obvious things which
nobody by any chance ever observes.

—Sherlock Holmes,
in *The Hound of the Baskervilles*

According to David, Watson and Holmes were in a cab ten minutes later, rattling along to Charing Cross Station. As for us, twenty minutes later, we stood outside the Palace Theatre, on the corner of Shaftesbury Avenue and Charing Cross Road.

David pointed. "That's it over there: 84 Charing Cross Road. Mr. Marks and his partner, Mark Cohen, specialize in old and rare books."

"Maybe Bertie and I can find a useful book on codes while you talk to Mr. Marks," Eleanor suggested.

The musty shop was full of old books, packed close together on tall wooden shelves. When Eleanor asked a clerk for titles on cryptology, he showed us to an area near a back stairway leading to an upper floor.

"This one looks interesting." Eleanor sat on the floor

to browse through it. LR plopped down beside her, sniffing hopefully at her knapsack.

"Wow, look at this: a whole section of books by Sir Arthur Conan Doyle," I whispered, scanning the titles on the shelves. "Some of them look ancient."

"Don't get distracted, Bertie," Eleanor told me. "And forget about buying one of those. They're probably first editions—that's the original version when it was first published."

I scowled at her. "I know that." Still, I felt a little out of place.

David had lingered behind to ask if Mr. Marks was available. "He's busy at the moment," I heard the clerk say. "His office is upstairs. May I tell him what this is about?"

"I'm just coming down now," said a voice. "What is it, young Frank?"

"There's a boy here to see you."

"Oh, hello, Mr. Marks. I'm not sure you remember me. I'm David Goodman and the Rosens are my foster family," David said.

I peeked out from behind my shelf to see David in conversation with a middle-aged gentleman with thinning hair. "You told us once that your son, Leo, got interested in codes by reading Edgar Allan Poe. I'm doing a school report on . . . on secret codes in detective stories. I'd love to ask Leo some questions."

At that moment, I heard footsteps on the staircase.

A voice called out, "Hullo. I'm Leo Marks. How can I help you?"

I couldn't see the newcomer at first. Then he moved into my line of sight. I held on to the shelf and gasped.

Because there was no doubt. No doubt at all.

Eleanor came up behind me, LR in her arms. She whispered, "What's wrong, Bertie? What is it?"

"That's him," I murmured.

"Who?"

"Q. Leo Marks is Q."

CHAPTER TWENTY-FIVE

Each student is given a personal identity
prefix and a security check, so that the
origin of the message can be established and
its authenticity guaranteed.

—*SOE Manual*

"What do we do now?" Eleanor murmured.

"Nothing. Let's just listen for a few minutes. Maybe they'll move so we can sneak out past him," I whispered. "Don't let LR bark or whine. I don't want him to notice her."

Or us, I thought.

From my hiding spot, I could see that the elder Mr. Marks had stepped away. David was spinning a very believable tale to Leo—at least I thought so.

"I want to mention different sorts of codes in my report," David was saying. "I've heard of a Caesar cipher and that one where you do the alphabet in reverse. What's it called again?"

"An Atbash cipher," answered Leo. "It derives its name from four Hebrew letters."

"Oh, of course. I should've remembered that: *Atbash* comes from the letters *aleph-tav-beth-shin*," David said. "*Aleph* is the first letter in the Hebrew alphabet, and it gets encrypted to *tav*, the last letter. *Beth* is the second, and gets encrypted to *shin*, the second to last. It's like saying *A-Z-B-Y*."

"That's right. Although it was originally used with Hebrew, we can do the same thing with the English alphabet. It's not a very robust cipher, however."

"That's why I wanted to ask you about other kinds," David said. I smiled. David was good at this. I poked my head out, then drew it back fast.

"We should leave," Eleanor whispered in my ear.

"In a minute," I murmured. "Let's just hear a little more."

"Of course, a substitution cipher doesn't even have to use letters," Leo was saying. "If you've ever read the Sherlock Holmes story 'The Adventure of the Dancing Men,' you know that Holmes cracks a cipher in which stick figures are substituted for letters."

"Oh, I know that story! He solves it by frequency analysis and the process of elimination, right?"

"Precisely," said Leo. "That's where you look for the most common two- and three-letter words and then try to discover patterns. For instance, the most common three-letter words in English are *the, and, for, was,* and so on. And then there are two-letter words such as *of, to, in, is,* and *it*."

"It seems like that method must take a long time," David said. I knew he must be thinking about Violette's last message. We didn't have much time left.

"It does get easier with practice," Leo told him. "Now then, another interesting cipher is the mixed-alphabet cipher with a key word."

"Mixed-alphabet cipher with a key word," David repeated. "What's that?"

"This one depends upon a key word or phrase, which is written out first as the beginning of the cipher alphabet. So if *DAVID* was your key word, *D* would stand for *A*, *A* would stand for *B*, *V* for *C*, and so on. The rest of the alphabet follows after the key word, skipping the letters you already used. It's easier to see it written out. Here, let's go to the desk in the back and I'll show you."

For a minute, I thought we'd be found out. I held my breath as they passed on the other side of the shelf. "Now's our chance, Eleanor."

Outside, we waited on the corner, out of sight. David joined us a few minutes later. "Why did you leave? I was looking for you. I would've introduced you to Leo. Gosh, he knows a lot! I definitely think we should try a key word cipher next."

"Go on, Bertie. Tell him," Eleanor urged.

"Tell me what?"

"Listen, David. We left for one reason. Leo Marks is Q."

"What?" he exclaimed. "What does that mean?"

"Come on." Eleanor pulled on David's sleeve. "Let's walk while Bertie explains."

"I think it might mean that Leo Marks and Violette work for the same organization. We know now that it's the SOE, with its office at the Inter-Services Research Bureau at 64 Baker Street," I began, navigating around other pedestrians so we could walk together—and not trip on LR's lead. "I bet Leo Marks is the code master Violette mentioned."

"Do you think he might also be the traitor, the double agent?" asked Eleanor.

David looked doubtful. "Leo is Jewish, like me. He wouldn't be helping the Nazis."

"It does seem unlikely. But then why didn't Violette go straight to him when she came to London?" Eleanor said. "Why did she want *me* to keep the notebook?"

"Maybe it would help to make observations like Sherlock would," David mused. "For one thing, Leo is about Violette's age. He's in his early twenties. So he's probably not high up in the organization. Maybe Violette figured he wouldn't be able to do much. And remember, Maurice told Violette he suspected the traitor was someone at the top."

Eleanor looked impressed. "Good point."

"Another thing. Even if Violette *wanted* to confide in Leo, she couldn't be absolutely sure. After what happened in France, she probably didn't feel she could trust anyone at the SOE. I mean, maybe Leo was working with the traitor or was under his control somehow.

More than anything, she wanted to keep her notebook safe," I said. "But I wonder . . ."

"Go on," David urged.

"Well, I wonder if somehow Leo Marks caught sight of Violette that afternoon. And then he followed her—and you too, Eleanor."

"Where did Violette ask you to meet her, Eleanor?" David asked.

"Well, we met in Portman Square. Then we made our way to Regent Street," Eleanor replied. "Portman Square isn't too far a walk from Baker Street."

"I wonder . . ." I tried to work it out. I wished I could be like Sherlock Holmes and magically spout the correct solution. "I wonder if Violette went to Baker Street before she met you, Eleanor. After all, she had been away in France for months. Maybe she just wanted to be sure the SOE office was still in the same location." As I spoke, I tripped over LR's lead and almost fell on top of her. "Sorry, girl."

"Here, let me take her so you can walk and talk at the same time," Eleanor teased.

I made a face but barely stopped for breath. "Here's what I think. When I followed Leo Marks to Baker Street, I saw him look out of a window. What if Violette had been watching the building from about the same spot I was? If he recognized her, he would have been—"

"Shocked," finished David, "because she was supposed to be in France."

I nodded. "And then he might have gone after her

and seen her with you, Eleanor. Violette probably suspected she was being followed as you were walking along Regent Street. And then after the air-raid began, she might even have ducked into Mill Street to hide."

"Or Leo Marks could have found her and confronted her." Eleanor's words spilled out. "Maybe she told him about the notebook. But when she said she no longer had it, he might have knocked her down. Bertie, did you notice if her pockets had been turned out, as if someone had searched through them?"

I thought that through. "I don't think so. But I suppose that theory could work. And Leo was running along Maddox Street in the same direction that you were. And I did see him the next day in Grosvenor Square. So I suppose it's possible he was following you, Eleanor."

David shook his head. "I . . . I just can't believe that Leo Marks is a double agent. I mean, think about it. He grew up in a *bookstore*. He reads Sherlock Holmes!"

That made Eleanor smile for just a minute. Then she sighed. "I feel like we're back where we started: We have to solve the last message and figure out Violette's trap."

"What else did Leo say about ciphers?" I asked David.

"Well, he did mention another possibility: a key word cipher with a mixed alphabet."

"That sounds pretty confusing," I said.

"It's actually a really interesting kind of cipher. You put a word or phrase at the beginning of the alphabet. And then, without repeating letters, you fill in the rest of the alphabet," David said.

Seeing our blank stares, he added, "Say your key word is *BLITZ*. You write those letters first, so *B* stands for *A*, *L* for *B*, *I* for *C*, *T* for *D*, and *Z* for *E*. Then you just keep going, starting with *A*, filling in the rest of the cipher alphabet, skipping the letters you already used in the key word. *A* stands for *F*, the next letter in the plain alphabet. Since you already used *B* in the key word, you don't use it again. So then *C* stands for *G* and so on. You just have to remember not to repeat any letters. So if your key word has any duplicates, like two *E*s or something, you skip the second one."

"I *think* I get it, but I'll have to see it written out to really understand it. Maybe we can work on that tomorrow afternoon," said Eleanor.

I wondered if we were all thinking the same thing: Tomorrow was Thursday. Time was running out fast.

"It feels like every time we get closer to finding the truth, more questions arise," said David.

"Here's another question," said Eleanor. "Now that we know Leo Marks is Q, should we confront him about following Violette, even though we don't know if he had anything to do with her disappearance?"

"No—at least not yet." I shook my head. "We don't want to ruin Violette's plans. For all we know, she's been in hiding and the trap is all set to be sprung."

"And if she's not . . . ," David began.

"If she's not, we need to figure out the trap and spring it ourselves," I said.

CHAPTER TWENTY-SIX

Shortly after the sirens wailed you could
hear the Germans grinding overhead. . . . You
could feel the shake from the guns. You could
hear the boom, crump, crump, crump, of heavy
bombs at their work of tearing buildings
apart. They were not too far away.

   —Ernie Pyle, American war correspondent in London

When we neared Berwick Street, David decided to head home. "Another history test tomorrow, Bertie," he reminded me.

"Mr. Turner works us harder than any other teacher," I told Eleanor. I wasn't sure how much history reading I'd do later. I had Violette's notebook with me. And I'd much rather work on the code than read about the Roman invasion.

"Well, Mr. Turner is demanding, but I like him," David put in. "He says that because we're living through a war against tyranny, we have a special responsibility."

"What kind of responsibility?" Eleanor asked.

"To learn from the past, understand the present, and change the future," David said.

Eleanor turned to face us. "Violette felt responsible

too. That's what made her decide to risk her life. We can't let her down." She put her hand out. "Let's put our hands together in a circle, like they do before a quest."

I picked up LR and we formed a circle to make our pledge: three hands and one furry paw.

I walked Eleanor to Hay's Mews, then said goodbye. LR and I meandered through Grosvenor Square, since I still had a few minutes before my shift. I walked around, thinking, while LR sniffed everything in sight. Sometimes she'd pounce on tiny crumbs from someone's lunch, her small, curly tail wagging a mile a minute.

We hadn't seen the sun all day, and now the gray skies were darkening to black. It felt eerie somehow. Maybe it was Eisenhower's headquarters looming before us. The blackout shades hid everything. But I knew it must be buzzing with activity inside.

"That's where Supreme Commander Eisenhower works. I bet your Scottish terrier friend Telek is there beside him," I told Little Roo.

I couldn't stop thinking about Violette and what was at stake. Warden Hawk had said this invasion would be the largest military operation in history, with thousands of troops landing on the coast of France on the first day. The landings would be followed by an onslaught of more soldiers, tanks, and planes, all focused on defeating Hitler's forces—and ending the war.

But what if things didn't go according to plan? What if the Germans were waiting for those soldiers as they spilled from their small boats onto the beaches? I wondered if anyone at military headquarters had an inkling that the invasion plan was in peril.

I was still standing there when it began. The sirens started up, their horrible wails crashing over me. LR began to shake and howl. For a minute, I hesitated. Should I run to make sure Eleanor and her grandmother were all right? No, they had a Morrison shelter in their home. They'd be fine.

I'd remembered to put my helmet in my school knapsack. I stuck it on my head before setting off along Brook Street to the command post. I didn't have my bicycle, but the wardens kept a few battered old bikes in the office. The most important thing was to get there.

The anti-aircraft guns had already gone into action. LR kept on howling, even as she trotted behind me. I raced past the red brick of Claridge's, with the British flag waving proudly over the entrance. I had to dodge several couples who seemed to be complaining that their dinner plans were being ruined.

I passed Master Humphrey's Clock Shop and slackened my pace to peer inside. I couldn't see any movement. I hoped Mr. Humphrey had a Morrison shelter. With his cane, he'd have a hard time rushing to a public shelter.

I was about to turn right on New Bond Street, which

would take me to the command post on Maddox, when a flare flashed behind me. Before I could take another step, a strong blast threw me to the ground. I felt the air being sucked out of my lungs. I reached for LR and held her close. She tried to wriggle away, back *toward* the blast.

Right away, I knew. The block behind me—and the clock shop—had taken a hit. And the old man with the fierce smile and the wild, bright hair was probably inside.

"Let's go back, LR!"

We were on the spot before anyone else. I guessed Mr. Humphrey lived above the shop. Maybe he had a Morrison upstairs, but if he'd been downstairs in the shop, he'd be in trouble.

I coughed as I came closer. The brick dust was thick and smoke filled my lungs. The door was gone, blown away. I stood in the empty space and yelled, "Mr. Humphrey? Mr. Humphrey, are you in here?"

Silence. I tried again.

I heard a moan. Little Roo whined and her small body quivered with anxiety. She pulled on the lead. "Lead me to him, girl. Mr. Humphrey! Can you hear me? Where are you?"

"Here. I'm here in the back office."

He was conscious, at least. I took a step. The dust was so thick I could barely breathe. I coughed again and felt glass crunch under my foot. Mr. Humphrey's lovely display cases had been shattered. *He's probably lost everything*, I thought. He was so proud of his shop, so determined to stick it out until the invasion. Until the end.

My eyes adjusted a little in the smoky gloom. I inched closer, but I wasn't sure I should go all the way through the shop. It might be safer to wait for help.

"Mr. Humphrey," I called again. I wanted to keep communication open. "My name is Bertie Bradshaw. I'm a civil defense volunteer. We met a few days ago in front of the bookshop."

"I remember." Mr. Humphrey coughed. The dust was thick. Then his voice came again, stronger this time. "So you've come to rescue me, have you?"

"Sir, if you're trapped under rubble, I should fetch help."

"No!" he cried. I could hear panic in his voice. "Oh, no. Don't leave me here, lad. We can get out. I just need someone to steady me."

"All right." I climbed over beams and piles of bricks and wood and shattered glass. My heart raced.

LR plunged ahead, her whole body straining against the lead. "Good work, LR. Lead me to him."

Suddenly I felt sick and light-headed, like I had before. I had to lean over and retch.

"I can't. I can't do this," I whispered. LR whined and stuck her warm muzzle in my face.

"You still coming?" Mr. Humphrey's voice sounded faint and tinny.

Woof! LR barked, as if urging me to follow her. I took a step. The whole shop was spinning now. I grabbed blindly, wildly, trying to stay on my feet. Instead, I lost my balance and fell hard on my knees, cutting my hand on some glass. I didn't feel it, though.

I put my head down. I didn't want to be sick again. But I was. I felt frozen.

"I can't move, Will! Come and get me. I'm scared."

But, somehow, this time—unlike that other day—I did move.

"It *is* you!" said Mr. Humphrey when I reached him. He held out one arm for me to grab. "Just pull hard. My cane's gone, lad, but I can make it."

I took a deep breath. "One, two, three!"

He groaned. But then he was upright. We picked our way toward the doorway. I heard him gasp at the ruined display cases and broken glass.

"I'm so sorry," I whispered. "I'm sorry about your shop, Mr. Humphrey."

Mr. Humphrey grunted. His hand gripped my arm. "I'll survive. Like I told you, young Bertie, the invasion is coming. The tide's about to turn." He repeated it like a prayer. "Yes, the invasion is coming, and I'm going to be here in London when it happens. No matter what."

It wasn't until later, sitting on the ground with a blanket over my shoulders, that I began to cry. Warden

Ita lowered his tall frame and put his arm around me. I shook a little, but gradually relaxed. LR snuggled in my lap.

"Why don't you tell me about it, Bertie?" Warden Ita said softly. "It's past time, I think."

I glanced up and met his dark eyes. He smiled a little. "I'm not asking just about what happened today. Warden Hawk told me your home got hit in the Blitz. I think you were inside?"

I buried my face in Little Roo's fur. I still felt a bit dizzy. I nodded. "Me and my brother, Will. Mum had run out to help a neighbor. She'd left Will in charge of me. He's two years older. I didn't like that.

"We had a back garden then, with an Anderson shelter in it. I was supposed to do what Will said if no one else was home. We'd even practiced it. But when the sirens went off that night, I was sleepy and grumpy. I was lying in bed and didn't want to get up. I wouldn't listen to him, and I didn't move fast enough. But Will wouldn't leave my side. And then the house got hit."

In the background, I could hear the buzz of conversation as people gathered to look at the blast site and talk in low murmurs. I heard Mr. Humphrey's voice too, louder than anyone else's. "I'm not getting in that ambulance. I need to board up my shop to prevent looting!"

A constable tried to reassure him. I turned my head and saw that it was George Morton. "Now, sir, I give you my word as a veteran of Dunkirk it'll get done, if I have to stay here until midnight and nail every board myself."

"Dunkirk, was it?" Mr. Humphrey said. "Now, let me tell you what I think about that military operation. . . ."

"Rather a feisty fellow, isn't he?" Warden Ita grinned, then turned back to me. "So . . . what happened after your house was hit, Bertie?"

"I . . . I was on one side of the room, and there was this sort of tunnel between Will and me. I was too scared to move. I wouldn't let him leave to get help. I *made* him come and get me. And then . . ."

Warden Ita's voice was low. "And then the rubble shifted?"

I nodded. "Yes, a wall collapsed; Will got trapped. I was fine, but it took them a long time to rescue him. We didn't know if he would make it."

"You can't blame yourself, Bertie," Warden Ita said quietly. "You were younger then."

"I was old enough to know better. I shouldn't have put my own brother in danger. I was old enough to be brave."

"Where's Will now?"

"He's in a rehabilitation hospital in Surrey. It's in the same town where my cousin Jeffrey's school moved after the war began. And it just so happens our grandmother lives nearby. So Mum has been staying with her to be close to Will. And I think maybe she couldn't bear London anymore."

"You didn't go?"

I shook my head. "Dad got a chance to be caretaker at Trenchard House, so I stayed with him. He goes out to visit a lot. I used to visit too, at first. But then . . . Will had to keep having operations. In the end, they couldn't save his left arm. At least he can write. But . . ."

"He's alive, and that's something," said Warden Ita.

"I know Mum blames me," I murmured. "And she's right to do that. It was my fault."

"You may always feel regret over what happened that night, Bertie. But that doesn't mean you can't move on with your life. You were brave tonight," said Warden Ita. "But it takes a different kind of bravery to talk to the ones we love, ask forgiveness, and move on. Sometimes all we can do is take one step at a time."

An ambulance driver called to Warden Ita and he walked over to her vehicle. The all clear had already sounded, though I'd barely realized it. I petted LR and stared at the rubble. Mr. Humphrey wasn't giving up. And I shouldn't either. I needed to keep trying to solve Violette's cipher. And I needed to make things better with Will. And Mum. I missed them both.

Warden Ita returned and reached out a hand to help me up. "Let's go back to the command post and have some tea. Then we'll get you home."

"What about Mr. Humphrey? Will he be all right?"

"He just left. It took some convincing to get him to go to the hospital, even for one night of observation. We'll contact his daughter." Warden Ita chuckled.

"As he was climbing into the ambulance, Mr. Humphrey said to thank you. And he had a message for you."

"What was it?" I asked, though I thought I could guess.

Warden Ita said, "He said to remind you that no one, not even Hitler, will force him out of London, because—"

"Because the invasion is coming and he intends to be here when it happens." And then I smiled.

CHAPTER TWENTY-SEVEN

It is a capital mistake to theorize before
one has data. . . . One begins to twist facts
to suit theories, instead of theories to suit
facts.

—Sherlock Holmes, in "A Scandal in Bohemia"

"That's two rescues this week, Little Roo," Warden Ita remarked as we walked to the command post. "You're a credit to the civil defense. We might have to recommend you for that new Dickin Medal for animal bravery."

"She'd probably be just as happy with a biscuit," I said. My head hurt and I felt achy all over. I held on to my knapsack. At least I hadn't lost the notebook.

"Warden Hawk rang, sir," Deputy Warden Esther told Warden Ita as we came in. "He's at a fire and wants you to meet him there. The address is on the desk. I'll take charge of this sweet lad. You look done in, Bertie."

Warden Esther settled me on the floor in a corner of the meeting room with a blanket over my shoulders. I rested my head against the wall and LR curled up beside me. Warden Esther brought me a cup of hot, sweet tea and a plate of biscuits.

"The constable at the reception desk at Trenchard House says your father won't be back until ten, but they'll send him here then."

"All right. Thank you."

It was quiet for a while. I thought about Mr. Humphrey. He might not be able to rebuild his shop. But he was determined to be around for the invasion.

"The invasion is coming," Mr. Humphrey had said. Everyone was saying it.

The whole city of London was breathing it in and out, like the first scented flowers of spring. The invasion was our hope. Our hope for an end to persecution and evil, an end to the war itself.

The invasion is coming. Violette had written that in her notebook too. It had been her very first sentence. In a way, it seemed like the invasion was the key to everything in our future. And then I remembered what Leo Marks had been talking to David about: a mixed-alphabet cipher using a key word or phrase. *A key word or phrase.*

Reaching into my knapsack, I grabbed the notebook, a pencil, and a piece of paper. Setting everything out on the floor before me, I wrote out the phrase, and then I filled in the rest of the alphabet, trying to remember David's directions. It took a couple of times, because at first I forgot that each letter of the key phrase could be used only once. Finally I had it:

PLAIN	A	B	C	D	E	F	G	H	I	J	K	L	M	N	O	P	Q	R	S	T	U	V	W	X	Y	Z
CIPHER	T	H	E	I	N	V	A	S	O	C	M	G	B	D	F	J	K	L	P	Q	R	U	W	X	Y	Z

Next, I turned to the first lines of Violette's final message:

bydtbnopuofgnqqnlfbyotbtdpfntandqbydn
qwflmodvltdenstphnndnxjfpniqsopopbylnjflq

B would be *M*. *Y* remains *Y*. *D* becomes *N*. *T* is *A*. I held my breath. Then I wrote faster and faster. It was like wiping off mist from a window. And finally these words emerged:

```
My name is Violette Romy. I am an
SOE agent. My network in France has
been exposed. This is my report.
```

I took a deep breath. *This is it,* I realized. *It's the key to her last message.* I couldn't wait to read it all. Maybe I could decode the whole thing tonight. My hands trembled with excitement.

Warden Esther stuck her head in. "Are you all right, Bertie? My goodness, lad, you look awfully pale," she said, coming toward me. Quickly I moved my knapsack to cover my work. She rested the back of her hand against my forehead in a couple of places. "Forgive me. My hand's a little cold." She smiled.

"My mum used to feel our foreheads for fever this way," I told her.

"And I'm sure she will again, Bertie. You seem to be fine. But there's a lot of bad influenza going around right now," she went on. "Mrs. Kathleen Clark, the rector's housekeeper at St. George's, was telling me she's barely left the sickbed of a patient in her care."

I listened, but all I could think of was decoding the rest of Violette's message. As she moved toward the door, I lurched to my feet and stuffed everything back into my knapsack. "Warden Esther, you know, I'm feeling much better. I'm just going to walk home and save my dad the trouble. Thank you for everything! I'll be fine."

Before she could stop me, I was gone, LR trotting beside me.

CHAPTER TWENTY-EIGHT

Some curious facts have been submitted to me
within the last twenty-four hours.

—Sherlock Holmes,
in "The Adventure of the Creeping Man"

THURSDAY

I was still in bed when the door flew open and Eleanor
and David burst in. LR hopped up and twirled in circles,
making excited, whiny noises in her throat.

My dad appeared in the doorway. "Sorry, Bertie. I
offered to make tea and discuss books, but they didn't
want to talk to me."

"Dad! I can't believe you'd let a girl in my room."
I scrunched the blankets up close under my chin. I
felt fuzzy and confused. "What time . . . Is it time for
school?"

"We've already *been* to school." Eleanor plopped
down on Will's bed, snatching up LR in her arms. "You,
apparently, have been sleeping most of the day. Your hair

looks like a bunch of red grass sticking up on top of your head."

I tried to flatten it. "Gee, thanks a lot, Watson."

"Bertie, I did try to wake you, but you were dead to the world," Dad put in. "I'll get you some tea."

"We both went from our schools to the command post, but you weren't there." David opened the blackout shade; I squinted as gray winter light flowed in. "Warden Ita said you saved Mr. Humphrey last night. Are you all right?"

"I cut my hand a little but it barely bled," I said. "And Little Roo deserves the credit. She led me to Mr. Humphrey." I paused and rubbed my eyes. "Hey, did I miss the history test?"

David grinned and pretended to be Mr. Turner. "'Since Mr. Bradshaw has chosen to absent himself, and the Roman invasion is his specialty, I'm postponing it until Monday.'"

I groaned. "Well, I couldn't have studied last night, anyway. . . ." I reached for a pile of papers under the bed.

"You were trying to crack the code for Violette's last message, weren't you?" asked Eleanor. Before I could answer, she said, "Bertie, I was up late thinking about the notebook too. I'm ready to go see my father. But I don't want to face him and explain everything alone. That's one reason we came over. I want us all to go."

"David and I will go with you . . . but maybe not quite yet," I said.

"Do you have a theory, Sherlock?" asked David.

"Not a theory—*answers*." I held out a piece of paper. "It's all here—well, almost all. And it was something Mr. Humphrey said that helped me unlock the cipher."

"You cracked it?" Eleanor's jaw dropped. "You might have started with that, Bertie."

"What sort of cipher is it?" David asked.

"It's the same kind Leo Marks told you about. The key phrase is *THE INVASION IS COMING*," I explained. "It makes so much sense: Violette started her notes that way too."

"Oh, Bertie, this is wonderful." Eleanor gave LR a big hug. "Did you decipher the entire message?"

I nodded. "It's just one page. I'll read it to you as we go."

"Where are we going?" they asked together.

"To spring Violette's trap, of course."

While they waited in the kitchen, I dressed quickly. Dad brought me some tea and toast on a tray. He stood uncertainly for a minute, and then perched on the edge of Will's bed.

"Bertie, I'm proud of what you did last night," he began slowly. "But from now on, you have to promise to leave the rescue work to the adults who are trained to do it. I know you feel guilty about what happened to Will. Risking your life won't change that."

"I know, Dad."

He pulled at the end of his mustache. LR jumped up beside him and snuggled close. He scratched behind her ears, and she leaned into his hand. *If LR was a cat, she'd be purring,* I thought.

Dad cleared his throat. "I reached your mother by phone this morning. We had a long talk."

I swallowed hard, wondering what was next.

"It made sense when Will was recovering from operations for him to be safely out of London," he went on. "But even though we don't know how long these new raids will continue, Mum and I agree that our family can't go on this way."

"Mum thinks it was my fault. You know she does," I said quietly. "She barely spoke to me for months and months afterward."

"She was half out of her mind with worry about Will. Remember, he almost didn't make it," said Dad. He sighed. "You and Mum do need to talk. She knows she has to try harder too, Bertie. She wants to be a mother to you both."

I opened my mouth to protest, then shut it again. I remembered what Warden Ita had said about taking things one step at a time. "All right, Dad. I'll try."

Dad smiled as he gave LR one last scratch. "Mum

misses you. So does Will. He's going to continue treatment and go back to school here in London. In a few days, they're coming home to stay." He grinned. "And I bet this little dog will be glad to have two more plates to lick after meals."

CHAPTER TWENTY-NINE

Great care is needed in using codes and
ciphers. One error may result in the message
being indecipherable and cause a serious loss
of time.

—SOE Manual

"Hold on a minute," I told David and Eleanor as we
left the flat. I handed Eleanor LR's lead and walked
over to the reception desk, where George Morton was
on duty.

"Uh, George. I just want to say . . . ," I began. "Well,
I'm glad you were there last night to help Mr. Humphrey."

George waved a hand. "All in the line of duty. He's
quite a character, ain't he?"

"He is. Also, can I ask . . . do you still have yesterday's newspaper?"

George sighed. "I was just about to catch up on the
sports news."

"I only need the personals."

"The personals?" He raised an eyebrow. "Whatever for?"

I struggled to come up with a reason. Then a real one popped into my head. "My brother, Will, is coming back to London to live. I want to . . . to find an old bicycle for sale. It might take him a while to learn, but I'll help him."

He grunted, dug out the right page, and pushed it toward me. "Here you go."

As I turned to leave, George called me back. He lowered his voice so David and Eleanor couldn't hear. "I have an old chum, a veteran of Dunkirk, who I'd like Will to meet. Once your brother's back, how about we have an outing? We'll treat you to tea at the big Lyons Corner House on Coventry."

I opened my mouth to say thank you, but George waved me off. "Go on, then, Bertie. Your friends are waiting."

We stepped outside and were instantly enveloped by a thick, stinky gray fog. I shivered in my old jacket and pulled my cap down low.

"Bertie, I'm bursting to know what's going on," exclaimed Eleanor.

"Let me check something first," I told David and Eleanor. The dense fog made it hard to read the tiny newspaper print, but it didn't take long to find what I wanted. I folded the newspaper and stuffed it into my pocket along with the last section of Violette's journal. "I was right. Let's go! Hopefully we can find our way there in this pea soup. We might have to wait until we get there for me to read you what I decoded."

David groaned, pulling his cap down lower against the damp, thick mist. "I'm as impatient as Eleanor. At least tell us where we're headed!"

I turned to David. "You're the real Sherlock expert here. What do you observe?"

David's dark eyes narrowed. "Well, let's see. We're headed south on Lexington Street, which isn't the way to the command post. And that newspaper must mean something."

"Oh, wait, I know!" Eleanor cried. "You discovered something related to Violette's trap." She stopped and pulled us both into a doorway. "I'm not going any farther until you read us the message and tell us what's going on."

Relenting, I took the sheet of newspaper and another folded piece of paper from my pocket. LR plopped down on my shoes, panting. "I'll read her report first. And then you'll know why we got the newspaper."

My name is Violette Romy. I am an SOE agent. My network in France has been exposed. This is my report.

This notebook contains evidence that I served loyally as an agent in the SYCAMORE network. It also points to evidence that a traitor in London has been working with the Nazis to aid their cause and send British agents into the hands of the enemy.

Under the instruction of my network leader, Maurice, I used our remaining funds to escape from France and return to London secretly. I do not know the real name or description of the double agent in the SOE network. But Maurice did reveal to me that he went by the code name TRAVELER.

In the next few days, I plan to lay a trap to draw TRAVELER into the open so that I may at least be able to identify him and convince officials in charge of the coming invasion to question and remove him.

I will use methods I learned for communicating in emergencies, along with my SOE code name, to attempt to trap him.

In the event that things do not go as planned, I am placing this notebook into trusted hands for safekeeping, and hope that it can be decoded and used to prosecute the traitor, whose actions threaten all of us.

Violette Romy

There was silence when I finished. Eleanor shook her head. "So now what? I'm not sure I understand how you figured out her trap."

"Remember when Violette was learning about the different types of coded messages?" I didn't wait for an answer, but barreled on. "Well, one way to communicate in an emergency is to place a personal notice."

David snapped his fingers. "And she says she planned to draw TRAVELER out using her own code name. And we know that is BOOK."

"Exactly. And," I added triumphantly, "that just

happens to match one of yesterday's personal notices in the newspaper."

Eleanor put her mittened hands to her cheeks. "Oh, wow."

"I think she probably placed the notice in the paper on Friday, Eleanor," I went on, unfolding the newspaper. "She probably had it run for several days, just to be sure her contact saw it."

David leaned over my shoulder. "Show us."

I ran my hand down the column of newspaper ads. "I guessed it would be in the lost and found section. And it was."

Eleanor and David bent their heads over the newspaper. I put my finger on the spot, and David read the notice aloud:

> If a traveler is searching for a lost book, Nelson will
> have it on Thursday, five o'clock in the afternoon.

"Oh, I don't get it," Eleanor said. "*Traveler* is the double agent, and *book* is Violette, but what is *Nelson*?"

"It took me a few minutes to figure that out," I admitted. "But my dad's always telling me about plaques and statues in London and—"

"Nelson's Column!" David thumped me on the back. "That has to be it."

Eleanor looked at us blankly. "Come on, tell me."

"Have you ever been to Trafalgar Square, near the National Gallery?" I asked her. "Well, the major landmark there is Nelson's Column. You can't miss it. It's a tall column with a statue on top. And on the bottom is a big granite base. It honors a famous navy hero, Admiral Horatio Nelson."

"If only Mr. Turner could hear you now, Bertie," David teased.

Ignoring him, I kept on. "So it seems pretty clear: This is how Violette is trying to lure the traitor. It took her weeks to reach England, so by now the SOE realizes it's missing an agent. She thinks TRAVELER will come looking for her, perhaps to find out what she knows and how much of a threat she might be to him."

Eleanor frowned. "But . . . but how will we know who he is if Violette doesn't show up herself?"

"We might not, unless it's Leo Marks," I admitted. "But I do have another idea to get him to identify himself." I reached into my knapsack and pulled out a book. "Eleanor, I think you should pretend to be Violette."

"Me?" she exclaimed. "But how? I'm not nearly as tall."

I handed her the book. "No, but if you sit on the steps at the base of Nelson's Column, the traitor might come close enough to get a good look. He—or she—might want to be sure you're not Violette. We can get a description, and once we find Violette, we can tell her. Hopefully she'll know who it was."

I knew there were several problems with my plan. For one thing, we had no idea how to find Violette. Or maybe the traitor had already seized her, and no one would show up. But it wouldn't do any good to jump ahead. *One step at a time.*

"Brilliant! And this fog will help," added David. "The person will have to get pretty close to tell if you're Violette or not."

"And don't worry, Eleanor," I assured her. "David and I will be nearby. If anything happens, we all run."

Eleanor nodded, drawing in a deep breath. "I'll do it."

"Let's go," I said. "It's almost time for our rendezvous with TRAVELER."

CHAPTER THIRTY

It is a hobby of mine to have an exact
knowledge of London.
                    —Sherlock Holmes, in "The Red-Headed League"

My heart pounded as we entered bustling Trafalgar Square. This could be it. As I scanned my surroundings, I almost felt like a real spy.

The National Gallery, with its large dome barely visible in the gray mist, seemed empty and deserted. I remembered going there with Dad, Mum, and Will when I was little. But when the war began, its precious paintings had been spirited away to safety.

"They still have concerts here sometimes at lunch," David said, gazing up at its tall columns. "My foster grandfather took me once. We had to wait in a really long queue."

Eleanor nodded. "And Nan and I often come to see the picture of the month."

"What's that?" I asked.

"After the Blitz died down, they started bringing one

painting a month out of hiding so people can visit it. They put it up during the day, and then store it overnight in some safe space."

"That sounds fun," I said. "A whole museum for one painting." I found myself wanting to tell Will about it. Maybe we could come again as a whole family.

Today, though, we weren't here for paintings or music.

The gray, soupy fog was so thick I couldn't make out Nelson standing on top of his tall column. I could barely see the four bronze lions that guarded the statue's granite base. David chose one in the front as his hiding spot. "I'll make myself invisible but keep my eyes peeled," he promised.

Before Eleanor ascended the steps, we had a whispered discussion. "I think you should sit on this front side too, facing the big fountain," I suggested. "Don't forget to listen for Big Ben."

The face of London's famous clock tower near Westminster wasn't lit, because of the war. But the bells still chimed. "LR and I will hide near a lion on the National Gallery side."

"All right. Don't worry, I'll be fine, Bertie." Eleanor reached into her knapsack and drew out a doughnut. "For Little Roo. Feed it to her slowly to keep her occupied."

I watched Eleanor stride confidently to the top step, just below one of the four bronze relief panels that decorated the column's base. She settled herself and tucked her hair under her hat, holding the closed book so it was visible.

LR and I moved into position. I pulled the feisty spaniel onto my lap and began to slip her bits of doughnut. I didn't want to take the chance of LR being recognized—especially if Leo Marks turned out to be the traitor.

Sunset was more than an hour away. In the summer, people often lounged on the steps to eat lunch. But Eleanor was almost alone on this cold winter day. The waiting seemed endless. As one face after another emerged from the mist, I found myself wondering who among the crowd could be a spy. And not just any spy—a corrupt one.

When the sound of chimes broke through the fog, I jumped. First I heard the four-note melody, and then Big Ben struck the hour: *bong bong bong bong bong*.

I waited. Nothing. No one came near Eleanor.

All at once, I felt LR stiffen in my arms. She whined and might have barked, but I put my hand over her muzzle. "Shh, quiet, girl."

Out of the corner of my eye, I saw what had captured LR's attention: a nondescript middle-aged man walking his dog. A handsome black dog, with a thick plumed tail.

I held my breath and ducked my head, pretending to

fish something out of my knapsack. But I kept watching him from under my cap. The man didn't turn my way. I saw him shoot a quick glance toward Eleanor. He hesitated for just a second, then kept walking. He didn't approach her. But he'd seen her. I knew it. He must've realized instantly that Eleanor wasn't Violette. Or maybe he'd been expecting someone else entirely.

The man was sharp—sharp enough not to fall for the trap.

But not sharp enough for us. Because LR and I recognized this pair. We'd seen them in front of the SOE office. I even remembered the dog's name: Hero.

The traitor's dog had given him away. TRAVELER might not realize it, but his dog was well named. He was a hero.

The man melted into the crowd and slipped out of view. I went around and tapped David on the shoulder, and we climbed up to sit beside Eleanor.

"No one came near me," Eleanor said. She swallowed hard and her eyes filled with tears. "I looked and looked for Violette, but I didn't see her anywhere. We don't know where she is. And on top of that, the trap failed."

"Bertie, does this mean we're giving up?" David asked quietly.

"Not a chance." I let LR down and gave her the last chunk of doughnut. "Once again, Little Roo has saved the day. She spotted TRAVELER."

"What? How?" David cried.

I told them what I'd seen. "I recognized the dog immediately. I'm not sure you noticed it when you were trailing me, Eleanor. But when LR and I tracked Leo to the Inter-Services Research Bureau on Baker Street on Saturday, we saw a beautiful black dog with a woman."

Eleanor shook her head. "I don't remember. I might have been across the street then. But how do you know TRAVELER has anything to do with the dog?"

"Well, the dog knew the way to the office. And the same man I saw today came out of the office and greeted his wife, who was walking the dog." I grinned. "I even know the dog's name: Hero. So while we may not know TRAVELER's name, Leo Marks will," I concluded with satisfaction. "Maybe it's time to go see him again."

"Oh, this is wonderful." Eleanor reached into her pocket, took out a handkerchief, and blew her nose.

I'd expected her to be more excited. "Are you feeling all right?"

"I'm still upset about Violette, I guess. And I started having chills sitting here," she admitted. "I hope I'm not getting sick."

Automatically, I reached out to touch her forehead with the back of my hand, just as Deputy Warden Esther had checked my temperature last night.

And in that instant, another memory came back to me. That tiny thing that had nagged at me since the night LR and I found Violette in the alley.

"Hullo, are you with us, Bertie?" David waved his

hand back and forth in front of my eyes. "You've got this faraway expression on your face."

"I just thought of something," I cried. "Something even more important than going to see Leo. We'll walk you home, Eleanor, but let's make a detour on the way. We'll be there in twenty minutes."

"Where's *there*?" David wanted to know.

"You'll see. Just follow me." It was all I could do to keep from running. But it was too foggy for that.

"This is the way to the command post," said Eleanor after a while. "Is that where we're headed?"

I shook my head. "Not quite. Just keep walking." I didn't stop until we reached the intersection of Maddox and Mill streets. "We're here."

"Wait a minute," Eleanor breathed. "Isn't this where you found Violette?"

I pointed to the "Food Waste for Pigs" bins. "Yes, behind there."

"I feel like Sherlock is about to reveal the solution to a case," David teased.

I grinned and took a breath. "When I was at the command post last night, Deputy Warden Esther felt my forehead to see if I was ill. But it wasn't until today, when I checked to see if Eleanor had a fever, that everything came rushing back to me. I don't think you're too warm, Eleanor, by the way." My words tumbled out. "You see, I remembered something I should've noticed at the time: When I touched Violette, her skin was warm. More than that, it was hot. Maybe because my hands were cold that night, I didn't think much about it. But then Deputy Warden Esther mentioned that there's a bad flu going around."

"I'm not sure I'm following," David said.

"Hear me out." I pointed across the street. "That building is St. George's rectory, a back annex to the big church, which has its main entrance on the next block. Well, Deputy Warden Esther just happened to mention that Mrs. Clark, the housekeeper at the rectory, said she's been caring for someone with a bad case of influenza."

"Someone with a bad case of influenza," Eleanor repeated. Her eyes widened. "And you think that someone might be Violette?"

"Maybe. And remember, Deputy Warden Esther has only been serving at our command post for a few days. The senior wardens are both so busy they probably never mentioned to her what happened on Friday night here on Mill Street," I mused. "She wouldn't have known to connect the report of a sick patient with the missing woman. But I think . . ."

Eleanor didn't wait for me to finish. She rushed over, ran up a few steps, grabbed the brass knocker, and let it fall on the red wooden door. *Knock! Knock!*

Almost immediately, the door swung open. A tiny woman with round pink cheeks and snowy white hair greeted us with a smile. "Good evening."

"Hello. Are you Mrs. Clark?" I asked.

"Why, yes, I'm Kathleen Clark. Can I help you?"

"We hope so," said Eleanor. "We're . . . we're looking for a friend. A friend who's fallen ill."

Mrs. Clark stepped aside and opened the door wider. "Well then, you'd better come in."

CHAPTER THIRTY-ONE

Combined with alertness of mind, the agent
should develop a good memory.

—*SOE Manual*

We followed the spry housekeeper into a neat sitting
room adorned with lace doilies, embroidered pillows,
and a woven rug of pale blue.

"What a pleasant room, Mrs. Clark," said Eleanor,
reaching out to shake hands. "Did you do all this needle-
work yourself?" Not waiting for an answer, she went on.
"I'm Eleanor Shea, from America. I'd like to present my
friends, Bertie Bradshaw and David Goodman."

Eleanor, I decided, could talk to anybody.

"Please sit down." Mrs. Clark beckoned us to a love
seat, where we huddled like pigeons on a rooftop. I held
LR tight on her lead. There were a lot of fragile things
she could knock over.

"I imagine you've come about Miss Smith," Mrs.
Clark was saying. "Dear Vi, as I've come to think of her."

Vi Smith! Was that our Violette? Before I could speak, Eleanor said smoothly, "How is Vi doing, Mrs. Clark?"

"Oh, much better, love. I discovered her quite by accident, you know. I found her after that horrid air raid last Friday when I went to empty meal scraps in the bins. Luckily, I was able to rouse Miss Smith and help her inside. Why, the poor girl might've frozen to death. . . ." She paused. "Though I did notice a strange thing. It seemed someone had covered her with a jacket."

"Um, that was me," I explained. "I'm a civil defense messenger. Actually, my little rescue dog here is the one who found Vi—er, Miss Smith. But when I returned with help, she'd disappeared. We thought maybe she'd gone home. And this street is mostly shops, so we didn't think that someone might have taken her in. . . ."

"We're quite hidden away here, that's true," said Mrs. Clark.

"Has she been very ill?" Eleanor asked softly.

"Oh, dear, yes. She can sit up now to drink some broth, but she was quite agitated when I refused to let her get out of bed today," replied Mrs. Clark, with a shake of her pearly curls. "I remember that terrifying flu epidemic in 1918, after the Great War, and I won't risk a patient of mine having a relapse."

"We're ever so grateful for your kindness." Eleanor beamed at Mrs. Clark. "Miss Smith is my tutor, you see. She was on her way home last week when she fell ill. My father and I have been at our wits' end searching for her. And, by chance, we heard the wardens on Maddox Street speaking about your extraordinary nursing skills. That's what led us here."

As their conversation continued, David turned to me and said under his breath, "How does she manage to spin these stories?"

"I think Eleanor's pretending to be a Mayfair society lady," I whispered back. "Like that clerk she met in the bookshop."

Mrs. Clark was getting to her feet. "Now, I can't let you see her for long, mind you. But I think she can be safely moved to your house this weekend, Miss Shea. I'll look forward to hearing from your father."

Eleanor smiled. For a minute, I thought she might curtsy. "And I know my father will wish to make a donation to St. George's church to show our gratitude."

Mrs. Clark led us down a hallway. Knocking gently, she opened a door. "Miss Smith, you have some young visitors. I'll bring in tea in a moment."

She closed the door and we stood silently, staring at the young woman in a pink dressing gown, sitting up in a narrow bed with a cluster of pastel pillows propped up behind her.

"Violette!" Eleanor rushed forward. And it was Violette. I knew it instantly too. Not just by her face and dark hair, but from seeing my own jacket hung neatly on a peg on the wall. I'd have to explain to Dad how I got it back. *Maybe,* I thought, *it's time to tell the truth.*

A few minutes later, Eleanor perched on Violette's bed, LR in her lap, while David and I sat awkwardly on straight-backed cane chairs, trying to balance plates with homemade scones and impossibly delicate teacups. David finally slurped his tea in one gulp and returned the cup to the tray Mrs. Clark had brought in and left on a side table.

Violette beckoned for David and me to draw our chairs closer. "Eleanor has told me of your impressive deciphering skills. So you know everything."

I could see LR eyeing the bed, so I kept hold of the lead. "Don't even think about it," I whispered in one furry ear. I didn't think Mrs. Clark wanted dirty paws on her pretty coverlet.

"Not quite," David told Violette. "Your last entry didn't give many details of your escape."

Violette smiled. "Well, it's a long story. I got out of France by crossing the Pyrénées into Spain on foot."

"How did you manage it?" I asked, fascinated. I'd never heard Violette speak in person before, but it was as if I already knew her from the notebook.

"First I took a train to a small village in southwest France. On the outskirts, I stopped at a farmhouse and met a woman and her son. Luckily, I had enough money to pay her to sew me a traveling outfit: riding jodhpurs and a knapsack. I traded my shoes for her son's old boots."

"Was crossing the mountains hard?" Eleanor asked.

Violette nodded. "But I trusted the woman's son to serve as my guide, and he knew that trail like the back of his hand. Luckily, the weather was kind to us. Once I reached Spain, I bribed the captain of a cargo vessel to hide me in his hold and bring me here. We sailed in a convoy of other ships. It was during the crossing that I began to feel ill. I rented a room, but only arrived the day before I met you, Eleanor."

"Did you stay hidden because you didn't want the British to detain you in prison, as a possible double agent?" I asked.

Violette nodded. "Yes, I knew that with the Nazis controlling the radio messages to London, they could easily smear my reputation and claim I was a collaborator. My only chance to unmask the real double agent was to stay free—and work undercover." She spread her hands in a gesture of despair and sighed. "But now what? I wasn't able to spring the trap today. I'm not sure he'll take the bait a second time. I've failed. And because of that, agents will be captured and killed. And the invasion itself—"

"No, you haven't failed," Eleanor broke in. She took Violette's hand. "Bertie found your hidden message in the newspaper. We've just come from Nelson's Column."

Violette looked up in surprise. "Oh, my goodness. What happened?"

I took up the story. "Eleanor pretended to be you. A middle-aged man with a handsome black dog showed up. He didn't speak to Eleanor, but I recognized him as someone I'd spotted before on Baker Street outside the Inter-Services Research Bureau, which we figure is just a cover for the real SOE offices inside."

Violette nodded.

I went on, "We think he *must* be the traitor, but we don't know his name."

"Do *you*?" David asked Violette. "I mean, do you know someone from your organization with a dog that looks like that?"

"*Je suis désolée*. I'm sorry; I don't. My training took place in the countryside," Violette told us. "I had one interview on Baker Street, and met with my code master there only once. I don't know who this man is."

After a minute, I spoke up. "Well, that's all right. Leo Marks will."

"Leo?" Violette said sharply. "Leo is the name of my code master. How do you know him?"

"My foster family knows his father," David told her. "And we went to Marks & Co, his bookstore, to see Leo. We asked him for advice about ciphers, because we had a hard time cracking your last message. But I pretended it was for school. I never said anything to him about you."

"Could Leo suspect you are here? Could he have been following you last Friday?" I put in.

Violette took a sip of tea. "I did go to Baker Street before I met you, Eleanor. I stood across the street. I thought perhaps, if Leo came out, I might approach him. I . . . I wanted to trust him. But then . . . then I decided to be more cautious and changed my mind." She stopped to cough and put down her cup. "We must talk quickly. Mrs. Clark will be back any moment to herd you away and make me rest. I'm afraid, *mes amis,* that I'm not a very good spy. I wanted TRAVELER to show himself." She picked at the coverlet with pale, thin fingers. "But after that, I wasn't so sure of my next steps. I thought I might go to your father, Eleanor, with my notebook as backup for my story. But how to get the highest military officials to listen, I still don't know."

Little Roo stood up on her hind legs and put her paws on me to beg for the last bite of scone. LR had been part of this adventure from the beginning. And looking at her, I got an idea.

"*Actually,* I might know a way we can get a meeting with the supreme commander himself," I said. "LR has friends in high places."

CHAPTER THIRTY-TWO

The main question was no longer which agents
were caught, but which were free. I ended my
report by saying as much.

—Leo Marks, in *Between Silk and Cyanide:
A Codemaker's War, 1941-1945*

WEDNESDAY, MARCH 1, 1944

"Who's growling?" said the man behind the desk.

There were a lot of people in the room. A lot of people and two dogs. It was probably one dog too many. At least Telek seemed to think so.

"Ah, it's my own Telek being a bad host, of course." The man grinned and pointed at me. "What's your spaniel called?"

"Her name is Little Roo, General Eisenhower. She rescues people after bombing raids." LR gave a little *woof!*

Telek might've been friendly outside in Grosvenor Square, but he didn't seem particularly pleased to have his personal kingdom invaded. I suppose you couldn't blame him. I mean, belonging to the supreme commander of the Allied Expeditionary Force, he was used to being top dog.

Eisenhower's aide, Harry Butcher, had already made introductions. Besides Eleanor, David, and me, Violette was there, of course. So were Leo Marks, Eleanor's father, and a serious, balding man introduced only as Sir Charles. I gathered he was Leo's boss and in charge of some, or all, of the SOE organization.

"Perhaps you can get us started, Harry," General Eisenhower said to his aide.

Harry Butcher stood. "Today, General, we're gathered to thank these young people for their role in preventing what might have been a serious breach of security for the coming invasion, and in helping save the lives of brave agents in the field."

"Very good." General Eisenhower gestured toward Sir Charles. "I've been assured that the culprit in this affair has been taken into custody. Is that right?"

Sir Charles shifted on his chair uncomfortably. "Yes, General. I take full responsibility for the delay. We are grateful to Violette for her courageous work. She provided valuable evidence from the field." He cleared his throat. "And . . . Leo had already called our attention to warning signs in coded messages that were being ignored by . . . by the traitor operating in our midst."

Leo picked at a nonexistent thread on his pressed trousers. Violette twirled a pair of gloves in her lap.

They said nothing, but I guessed it was hard for them to stay quiet.

Violette had risked her life to bring TRAVELER to justice. And Leo had told us he'd tried for weeks to convince his superiors (including TRAVELER himself) to pay attention to the absence of security checks in agents' messages. He didn't believe it was carelessness: He'd trained agents like Philippe and Violette well. TRAVELER had tried to discredit Leo. But in the end, Leo had been proven right.

Everything had come together quickly since the day we'd discovered Violette. On Sunday, she'd moved from the rectory to stay with Eleanor and her family. That afternoon, David, LR, and I had walked to the bookstore on Charing Cross Road to find Leo. Luckily, he was there visiting his father.

"Wait a minute. I've seen you and your little spaniel before, haven't I?" Leo asked me.

I nodded. "Yes, after the air raid last Friday. I think you might have been following someone then: a young woman?"

"How do you know that?" The blood drained from Leo's face. He grabbed our arms, herded us behind a bookshelf, and whispered, "I thought I glimpsed her that day. But she's not supposed to be here. . . . Is she safe?"

"Yes," David declared. "It's rather a long story, but if you're free, we'll take you to her."

In a way, it was a relief to bring other people into the mystery. Dr. Shea had assured Leo and Violette that they could speak with him in confidence, and that his American organization, the OSS, worked closely with British groups like the SOE on Baker Street.

Dr. Shea even made a joke about it. "I had one meeting at your offices, and walked around looking for a sign that said *SOE*. It was only when I checked the address that I realized you're hidden behind that cryptic sign on the building that says *Inter-Services Research Bureau*. I wonder who came up with that!"

Leo grinned. "We couldn't exactly say *Baker Street Irregulars*." Then he held Violette's hand for a long moment. "I am glad you're alive. I happened to glance out my office window and thought I must be dreaming. You were supposed to be in France. I began following you to be sure, but you vanished when the sirens went off."

Violette nodded. "I almost trusted you, Leo. I wanted to. But I decided to try to lure the traitor into the open on my own first. Then I thought I would talk to you or Dr. Shea. I gave the notebook to Eleanor to be kept safe—in case . . . in case something happened to me.

"But, as you know, these young people proved to be better spies than me. During the raid that night, I began to feel faint and sick. Eleanor had sprinted ahead.

So when I saw those bins on Mill Street, I decided to crouch behind them to catch my breath. Foolishly, I thought I might hold the tin lid of the garbage can over my head for protection in case a bomb fell nearby. But I didn't even have the strength to lift the lid. I fainted dead away! When I woke up, Mrs. Clark was helping me inside the rectory."

Leo said, "I thought you were with someone else, Violette, but I never got a good look at Eleanor. Once the air-raid sirens went off, it was pretty chaotic. I kept running along Maddox Street toward Grosvenor Square because I didn't realize you had gone into Mill Street."

Leo turned to me. "And, in fact, I did take your advice and slipped into a shelter."

"Did you go to Grosvenor Square to look for Violette the next day?" I asked.

Leo nodded. "I had the vague notion I might run into her, since that seemed to be the direction she was heading. I saw you and your dog then, Bertie, but I didn't know anything about the notebook."

"So I guess it was all in my head that you were following me that afternoon," I said ruefully. Although if I hadn't tracked Leo to Baker Street, I'd never have known that the man with the dog was TRAVELER.

Dr. Shea had listened to the whole story so far in surprised silence. But his jaw dropped as Eleanor revealed how the three of us had deciphered the notebook and sprung Violette's trap for the traitor.

"This is incredible, Eleanor," said Dr. Shea. "You three have done some exceptional detective work. But why didn't you come to me sooner?"

I was about to speak up, but I stopped myself. This was Eleanor's question to answer. She shrugged. "I don't know. You've been so busy."

"I'm sorry, my dear. It's one reason why I didn't want you to come to London," he said.

"No!" Eleanor's head shot up. "I'm glad I'm here, Father. I'd hate boarding school. And I love living here. I just want to . . . to be taken seriously."

He nodded solemnly. "I'll do better. Once the invasion is over, we'll all breathe a sigh of relief, I think. It may not be the end of the war, but it will be the beginning of the end. And, Eleanor, my dear, I want you to know that I consider you, like the woman you're named for, a force to be reckoned with—and I love you for that."

"Always Eleanor," I whispered, poking Eleanor in the ribs.

Dr. Shea paused, then addressed us all. "And now, you Baker Street Irregulars, do you have an idea for what should happen next?"

"Actually, we do, sir," I said. "I think I have a connection that can bring this information about the traitor to the highest levels of the military—with your help."

Dr. Shea looked amused. "I see. What would you like me to do?"

"I wonder if you'd be willing to make a call to Commander Harry Butcher and ask him to meet you outside headquarters at Grosvenor Square."

"Eisenhower's aide?" asked Eleanor's father, with a low whistle. "That *is* the top!"

I grinned. "You can tell him Telek's friend would like to meet again."

Dr. Shea had indeed called Harry Butcher to make our case. After that, there'd been a flurry of calls and secret meetings (to which we kids weren't invited). But now we all were here.

As soon as I'd mentioned that LR was a rescue dog, Supreme Commander Dwight D. "Ike" Eisenhower had risen from his desk, walked over, and bent down to give her a treat: a American Red Cross doughnut! Telek had whined, aghast that a guest had been served before him.

The supreme commander turned to me. "Well, young man, I'd like to hear a little more about how you three solved this mystery and helped ensure that our great endeavor will remain a secret."

I was silent a moment. David whispered, "Go on, Sherlock." Eleanor nodded encouragement. I took a breath and began to tell the tale.

"I wasn't thinking about becoming a spy that night. . . ."

CHAPTER THIRTY-THREE

Soldiers, Sailors and Airmen of the Allied
Expeditionary Force!
  You are about to embark upon the Great
Crusade, toward which we have striven these
many months. The eyes of the world are upon
you. The hopes and prayers of liberty-loving
people everywhere march with you.

                    —General Dwight D. "Ike" Eisenhower,
      Supreme Commander of the Allied Expeditionary Force,
                    in his Order of the Day on June 6, 1944

TUESDAY, JUNE 6, 1944

"Bertie, wake up and listen!" Will's urgent voice roused me in the darkness of our room.

I rolled over, pulled LR close, and mumbled, "Listen to what?"

"Planes," he said. "I heard planes. I wonder if it means the invasion is happening today."

"Maybe Jeffrey was right," I said, sitting bolt upright. Of course Jeffrey was right. "Did you hear him predict it would happen this week when he was here on Sunday? He said all the soldiers were gone from the camp near his school."

"They were probably sent to the south of England. By now they're on their way across the Channel," Will said. "Hey, let's listen to the BBC news on the radio."

Will and I wanted to eat breakfast in our sitting room, next to the radio, but Mum wouldn't hear of it. "We'll turn the volume up a bit and you can sit right here in the kitchen," she said, setting out plates of toast, sausage, and those dreaded powdered eggs.

Ever since she'd come home, my mother had embarked on a plan to "re-civilize" me. It involved regular haircuts, more homework, and making me eat better. "What did you and your father live on?" she'd exclaimed when she arrived. "Tea and toast?"

"Don't forget powdered eggs," Dad had put in. "Mine are the best."

I'd groaned. "The best were the doughnuts Eleanor fed me. Doughnuts are now LR's favorite food."

"Well, I'm glad someone else is getting smothered by Mum's love," Will had teased. Then he'd gone over and kissed her on the cheek. "I couldn't have gotten well without you, Mum."

She'd frowned. "You must be sweetening me up for something, Will Bradshaw. What's going on?"

"Nothing much." Will had grinned. "Well, except Bertie found an ad for a free bicycle in the newspaper. It needs work, but once I learn to ride one-handed, Warden Hawk said he'd take me as a civil defense messenger."

In the end, the four of us traipsed into the sitting room when the BBC news came on at eight o'clock, breakfast plates in hand, much to the delight of LR.

"Here is the eight o'clock news for today, Tuesday the sixth of June, read by Frederick Allen," the announcer's voice declared. "Supreme Allied Headquarters have issued an urgent warning to the inhabitants of the enemy-occupied countries living near the coast. The warning said that a new phase of the Allied air offensive had begun. . . ."

"It must be coming! This must be the day," I cried. "The invasion is happening at last."

David and I went straight to talk to Mr. Turner when we got to school. "I think this is the day. Come to my classroom during lunch," he told us. "I'll put the radio on."

Sure enough, there was a special midday bulletin:

"D-Day has come. Early this morning, the Allies began the assault on the northwestern face of Hitler's European fortress. The first official news came just after half past nine, when Supreme Headquarters Allied Expeditionary Force—usually called SHAEF, from its initials—issued Communiqué Number One. This said: 'Under the command of General Eisenhower, Allied naval forces, supported by strong air forces, began landing Allied armies this morning on the northern coast of France.'"

After school, I stopped home to fetch LR, then joined David, Will, and Eleanor at the command post, where a large group had gathered around a radio, eager for the latest news.

We stayed all afternoon. The wardens were joined by volunteers and neighbors who stopped by to hear the news. Once, a little boy cried, "Mummy, look! There's the doggie that rescued us." Needless to say, LR got a biscuit.

And then, after one radio update, Warden Hawk gave a hoot of joy and slapped his knee. "Did you hear that? The attack was a tactical surprise. They did it! Eisenhower managed to keep the largest military endeavor in history, with thousands of planes, boats, and soldiers, a secret."

Will turned to David, Eleanor, and me and whispered, "And luckily, the supreme commander had help from the three of you."

LR stuck her muzzle into the air and barked. *Woof!*

"Not three—four." I reached down to hug my dog. "We can't forget Little Roo."

EPILOGUE

We had a going-away and birthday party combined. Unfortunately, not everyone could make it. We knew Leo Marks was busy. And we figured Telek, the supreme dog, might be in France, helping his master inspect troops after their courageous and successful assault on the beaches of Normandy on D-Day.

Dr. Shea and Eleanor were heading home. Eleanor's father would go back to teaching in the fall. But he'd promised Eleanor they'd come visit next summer.

He launched the festivities with a lemonade toast. "Happy birthday to my brilliant daughter, Eleanor, who was born on a historic day: July fourth. Although our two nations separated, when we come together as allies on the battlefield—or in the pursuit of truth and justice—we are unbeatable."

"Hear, hear!" We all raised our paper cups.

"My birthday is historic in more than one way: Thomas Jefferson and John Adams died on that day," Eleanor said with a grin. We all groaned. "I guess they were sort of responsible for our two countries breaking up in the first place. . . ."

I glanced at Dad. "Well, this is a good place for our picnic, then. John Adams once lived on Grosvenor Square."

David whistled. "Mr. Turner would be impressed, Bertie."

"Bertie might even turn out to be a history buff like you, Dad," Will added.

"He might at that," Dad said. "But I have to thank you, Warden Hawk and Warden Ita, for helping my son learn to be more responsible and, shall we say, less forgetful."

Warden Hawk grinned and went back to throwing a ball for Little Roo. Warden Ita flashed his beautiful smile. "We're glad to have both your sons as volunteers now."

After we sang, Mum helped Eleanor cut the apple pie she'd made for the occasion. "Eleanor, could you please take these pieces to Mrs. Clark from the rectory and to your grandmother?" Mum asked. "Bertie, these are for

Warden Esther and Mr. Humphrey." She smiled down at Little Roo and planted a kiss on my cheek. "And, of course, our little heroine gets her own piece."

As we walked across the now-green grass in Grosvenor Square, Eleanor said softly, "Your mom is nice, Bertie. Are things better?"

I smiled a little. "Warden Ita once told me to take things one step at a time."

I wished I could jump ahead to a time when Mum and I were always easy with each other. But we were trying. She kissed me good night. And sometimes, if Will was reading Holmes aloud, she sat at the foot of my bed, stroking Little Roo's head with one hand and rubbing my feet with the other.

"Good night, my boys," Mum would say on those nights. "And you too, Little Roo."

Sometimes I also wished I could leap to a time when the war was over and London would never again face another raid. The Little Blitz bombing raids had stopped. But starting a week after D-Day, we'd had something new and terrifying to deal with: V-1 flying bombs. They were pilotless missiles launched from positions the Germans still held in France, and arrived without warning. And though we didn't know it then, they would continue for months. We called them doodlebugs, or buzz bombs.

But Warden Hawk and Warden Ita weren't discouraged. They would keep fighting for the people of London.

We could sense that it was only a matter of time before the war would end.

As for other guests, there was one young constable present, but it wasn't Jimmy. He didn't live at Trenchard House now. He wasn't even a policeman anymore.

My suspicions about Jimmy had been wrong—he hadn't been Violette's boyfriend after all. But my cousin Jeffrey had been right to distrust him. Not only had Jimmy been mean to LR, he was caught accepting bribes from criminals. Dad caught him and received a special commendation.

"Are you going to become a detective now, Dad?" I'd asked.

"Bertie, I turned down a detective inspector position before the war," he'd told me. "I thought I could do more good training young policemen to serve the community. I wanted to be on the streets with the people of London. I know that might come as a disappointment to you."

I'd shaken my head. "Before . . . before, I might have thought that. But not anymore."

Dad had rested his hand on my shoulder. "We'll see what happens when the war ends. I might need a promotion to help us get our own house again."

• • •

Will, Jeffrey, and David were almost too busy to eat their pie: They were arguing the merits of their favorites of the fifty-six Sherlock Holmes stories.

Will and David were still the Sherlock experts. David read a lot. And he worked hard too. He'd told me once that staying busy helped him get through the worst days of missing his parents. And this summer he was helping not only in his foster family's shoe store but also in Leo's father's bookstore at 84 Charing Cross Road.

" 'A Scandal in Bohemia' is definitely the best Sherlock Holmes short story," Will was saying.

"No way," David argued. "I read that Sir Arthur Conan Doyle himself liked 'The Adventure of the Speckled Band' best."

"Forget the stories. The best is his novel *The Hound of the Baskervilles*," Jeffrey proclaimed.

Eleanor added her opinion. She had recently decided to read the Holmes stories from beginning to end in chronological order. "I know which one should be Bertie's favorite: 'The Red-Headed League.' "

"Very funny," I told her. "You're lucky I don't pour this lemonade on your head."

When I walked past Violette and George, I heard him ask, "So I hear you love to dance. Would you . . . would you consider . . ."

Violette smiled. "I'd love to go to a dance with you sometime, George."

The most surprising new friendship, however, wasn't

between Violette and George. Mr. Humphrey, no worse for wear after his ordeal, was planning to move in to the extra flat in Eleanor's grandmother's house once Eleanor and Dr. Shea returned to America.

"My daughter, Lydia, wants to keep me penned up in the countryside like some sort of old nag. Too many chickens! Too noisy. Give me London any day," the old man declared. "I was here for the invasion. Next is the victory parade. And thanks to Bertie and one small, brave dog, I'll be around to see it."

Little Roo didn't bark. She was too busy eating her apple pie.

Spy Practice Number Four

MIXED-ALPHABET CIPHER
USING A KEY WORD OR PHRASE

r d b k g x m s a m p p z b t e k c r d e q l m m g !

This is the type of cipher Violette used for her last message. In this kind of substitution cipher, a key word or phrase is used to generate the cipher alphabet. The key word comes first, at the beginning of the alphabet. After that, the rest of the letters are listed in alphabetical order, excluding those already used in the key.

Each letter in the key word is used only once. So if your key word is *ZOO*, *A* becomes *Z* and *B* becomes *O*. Then you run out of letters in the key word, and the whole rest of the alphabet doesn't change—so *ZOO* is obviously not a strong key word. Longer key words and phrases, especially ones that include letters from the end of the alphabet, work better.

Hint: The key word to unlock this message is the five-letter word used to describe the German bombings of London and other English cities during World War II.

ANSWERS TO CIPHER MESSAGES

Spy Practice Number One

SUBSTITUTION CIPHER

The supreme commander of the Allied Expeditionary Force was Dwight D. "Ike" Eisenhower. Since his nickname was Ike, this cipher alphabet begins with the letter *I*.

```
q n g w c i z m j m q v o e i b k p m l q b q a m a a m v b
q i t n w z g w c b w j m i e i z m w n q b
```

ANSWER: If you are being watched, it is essential for you to be aware of it.

There are several online resources that can help you encrypt plain text and decode encrypted text. Of course, these tools weren't available in 1944. Here is a website you can explore: practicalcryptography.com/ciphers.

Spy Practice Number Two

CAESAR (SHIFT) CIPHER

Operation Neptune (the code name for the assault on Normandy) took place on June 6, 1944. In this type of substitution cipher, the shift equals the number of the month plus the date. That means we shift a total of twelve letters: six for June, the sixth month, plus six for the day of the month. So the first letter of the cipher alphabet is *M*.

kagwz aiyky qftap eimfe azetq dxaow taxyq e

ANSWER: You know my methods, Watson. —Sherlock Holmes

Spy Practice Number Three

ATBASH CIPHER

In this cipher, the alphabet is reversed.

blfix levir hgsvo ruvds rxsbl flfgd
ziwob ovzwr mliwv iglxl mxvzo gsviv
zokfi klhvl ublfi kivhv mxvzm wgsvv
ckozm zgrlm dsrxs blftr evlub lfikz
hgzmw kivhv mghlv nzmfz o

ANSWER: Your cover is the life which you outwardly lead in order to conceal the real purpose of your presence and the explanation which you give of your past and present. —*SOE Manual*

Spy Practice Number Four

MIXED-ALPHABET CIPHER
USING A KEY WORD OR PHRASE

The German bombing campaign against Britain in 1940–1941 was known as the Blitz. So the key word for cracking this message is *BLITZ*.

r d b k g x m s a m p p z b t e k c r d e q l m m g !

Here is the key:

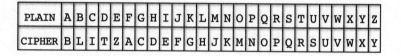

PLAIN	A	B	C	D	E	F	G	H	I	J	K	L	M	N	O	P	Q	R	S	T	U	V	W	X	Y	Z
CIPHER	B	L	I	T	Z	A	C	D	E	F	G	H	J	K	M	N	O	P	Q	R	S	U	V	W	X	Y

ANSWER: Thank you for reading this book!

SOURCE NOTES

The Special Operations Executive (SOE) was a World War II British organization that recruited ordinary men and women to conduct espionage and sabotage in Nazi-occupied countries. Its headquarters were located on Baker Street in London. SOE training lectures have been collectively published as *Special Operations Executive Manual: How to Be an Agent in Occupied Europe* (London: William Collins, 2014), abbreviated here as *SOE Manual*. Excerpts are used by permission of the National Archives, London, England, under the terms of the Open Government License.

Sherlock Holmes quotations from the novels and short stories of Arthur Conan Doyle have been accessed online through Project Gutenberg: gutenberg.org.

* * *

Part One. "The agent, unlike the soldier . . .": *SOE Manual,* 13.

Chapter One. "You see, but you do not observe . . .": Doyle, Arthur Conan. "A Scandal in Bohemia," *The Adventures of Sherlock Holmes,* 1892.

Chapter Two. "Never trust to general impressions . . .": Doyle, A. C. "A Case of Identity," *The Adventures of Sherlock Holmes,* 1892.

Chapter Three. "[The agent] should not only . . .": *SOE Manual,* 15.

Chapter Four. "The agent . . . has only . . .": ibid., 13.

Chapter Five. "If you follow conscientiously . . .": ibid., 13.

Chapter Six. "I may be on the trail . . .": Doyle, A. C. "The Adventure of the Beryl Coronet," *The Adventures of Sherlock Holmes,* 1892.

Chapter Seven. "Do not walk or hang about . . .": *SOE Manual,* 49.

Chapter Eight. "If you suspect that you . . .": ibid., 49.

Chapter Nine. "The watcher should always . . .": ibid., 48.

Part Two. "Come, Watson, come! . . .": Doyle, A. C. "The Adventure of the Abbey Grange," *The Return of Sherlock Holmes,* 1904.

Chapter Ten. "It seemed to me . . .": Roosevelt, Eleanor. "My Day": www2.gwu.edu/~erpapers/myday/displaydoc.cfm ?_y=1942&_f=md056326.

Chapter Eleven. "The agent should merge . . .": *SOE Manual,* 15.

Chapter Twelve. "Undaunted by smouldering debris . . .": PDSA Dickin Medal, pdsa.org.uk/what-we-do/animal-awards -programme/pdsa-dickin-medal.

Chapter Thirteen. "The agent should not . . .": *SOE Manual,* 15.

Chapter Fourteen. "Surveillance is the keeping . . .": ibid., 45.

Chapter Fifteen. "A cipher is a method . . .": ibid., 122.

Part Three. "To the question why . . .": Kramer, Rita. *Flames in the Field: The Story of Four SOE Agents in Occupied France* (New York: Penguin Books, 1996), 247.

Chapter Sixteen. "You should always . . .": *SOE Manual,* 48.

Chapter Eighteen. "Good cryptographists are rare indeed.": Poe, Edgar Allan. "A Few Words on Secret Writing," *Graham's Magazine,* July 1841, 19:33–38. eapoe.org/works/essays /fwsw0741.htm.

Chapter Nineteen. "The agent must not leave about . . .": *SOE Manual,* 16.

Chapter Twenty. "Never relax your precautions . . .": ibid., 13.

Chapter Twenty-One. "The introduction of an agreed name . . .": ibid., 124.

Part Four. "When you have eliminated the impossible . . .": Doyle, A. C. *The Sign of the Four,* 1890.

Chapter Twenty-Three. "I thought that I could . . .": Cornioley, Pearl Witherington. *Code Name Pauline: Memoirs of a World*

War II Special Agent (Chicago: Chicago Review Press, 2013, 2015), 33.

Chapter Twenty-Four. "The world is full of obvious things . . .": Doyle, A. C. *The Hound of the Baskervilles,* 1902.

Chapter Twenty-Five. "Each student is given . . .": *SOE Manual,* 121.

Chapter Twenty-Six. "Shortly after the sirens wailed . . .": Pyle, Ernie. *Ernie Pyle in England* (New York, R.M. McBride & Company, 1945), 22. Print on demand reissue.

Chapter Twenty-Seven. "It is a capital mistake . . .": Doyle, A. C. "A Scandal in Bohemia," *The Adventures of Sherlock Holmes,* 1892.

Chapter Twenty-Eight. "Some curious facts . . ." Doyle, A. C. "The Adventure of the Creeping Man," *The Case-Book of Sherlock Holmes,* 1923.

Chapter Twenty-Nine. "Great care is needed . . .": *SOE Manual,* 122.

Chapter Thirty. "It is a hobby of mine . . .": Doyle, A. C. "The Red-Headed League," *The Adventures of Sherlock Holmes,* 1892.

Chapter Thirty-One. "Combined with alertness of mind . . .": *SOE Manual,* 15.

Chapter Thirty-Two. "The main question was . . .": Marks, Leo. *Between Silk and Cyanide: A Codemaker's War, 1941–1945* (New York: Free Press, 1998), 124–125.

Chapter Thirty-Three. "Soldiers, Sailors and Airmen . . ." Eisenhower, Dwight D. "Order of the Day." National Archives. archives.gov/historical-docs/todays-doc/?dod-date=606.

Author's Note. "The people of the world . . ." Ekpenyon, E. Ita. *Some Experiences of an African Air-Raid Warden.* westendatwar.org.uk/documents/E._Ita_Ekpenyon _download_version_.pdf.

AUTHOR'S NOTE

"The people of the world are divided into two
camps, one camp trying to enslave the world,
the other camp fighting to have peace and
freedom in the world."

—E. Ita Ekpenyon, in *Some Experiences
of an African Air-Raid Warden*

How I Became a Spy is a fictional story inspired by events during World War II. While some actual historical figures do appear in the book, all their actions and dialogue are entirely invented and should be considered fiction, with no relation to real people.

Historical Background

The world was at war. Hitler's Nazi Germany had invaded other nations, inflicting terror, torture, and death on innocent people, especially Jews. Great Britain had been at war with Germany since September 3, 1939. Londoners had endured food rationing, blackouts, and bombing raids collectively known as the Blitz in 1940 and 1941. Attacks began again in 1944, in a series of operations that has come to be known as the Little Blitz.

The United States had entered the worldwide conflict in 1941 as an ally of Great Britain. As the future of free democratic societies hung in the balance, Britain and America joined forces to begin secret preparations for the largest military operation in history: Operation Overlord. Its goal was to invade Hitler's "Fortress Europe" and defeat Germany at last.

Much would depend on the success of the first day of that battle, when 156,000 Allied troops would cross the English Channel and fight for a toehold in France. The code name for the landings was Operation Neptune. It was one of the most crucial secrets of World War II. The Nazis must not find out when it would take place, or exactly where troops would land.

The Special Operations Executive

Thousands of ordinary people took part in the fight against Nazi Germany. In England, an organization called the Special Operations Executive, or SOE, was formed. Its agents were known as the Baker Street Irregulars, after the street urchins who assisted the famous fictional detective Sherlock Holmes. The SOE main office was at 64 Baker Street, marked by a sign that read INTER-SERVICES RESEARCH BUREAU. Visitors can find a plaque there today.

The SOE trained men and women with no previous experience to become secret agents. After training, many were dropped by parachute into countries occupied by Nazi Germany, including France, Denmark, and the Netherlands. There they undertook dangerous acts of sabotage and resistance.

Unfortunately, as in our story, several networks were compromised when the Nazis captured agents and radio operators but continued to send radio messages. Yet even when messages arrived without the proper security check codes, the London office of the SOE assumed that these were simple coding mistakes made by agents in the field. As a result, a number of British agents were captured and killed. Leo Marks, an SOE code maker, is credited with discovering this pattern in the Netherlands. While no double agent was uncovered, controversy over this tragic situation continued long after the war.

AUTHOR QUESTIONS & ANSWERS

What inspired you to write this book?

I love mysteries, spy stories, history, and anything to do with London. I'm also interested in World War II and have written several nonfiction books about it, including one about D-Day and one about the SOE in Denmark.

I was able to visit London while writing another historical fiction book, *The Great Trouble,* which takes place on Broad Street (later Broadwick Street) in 1854. I wanted Bertie's father to be a policeman. When I discovered that Trenchard House, a police apartment building, was located on Broadwick Street in the 1940s, I knew exactly where Bertie should live.

What did an air-raid siren sound like?

You can hear a WWII British air-raid siren and the all-clear signal that followed on YouTube: youtube.com /watch?v=erMO3m0oLvs.

Was there really a Little Blitz in the winter of 1944?

Yes. Although the most intensive period of bombings in London occurred primarily in 1940 and 1941, attacks began again in January of 1944. However, while I've followed the general timeline of raids during this time, I have fictionalized the command post, as well as the actual bombing incidents and their locations that appear in the story.

Do you have a dog named Little Roo?

Not exactly! But I do have a brown-and-black cocker spaniel named Rue, after a character in *The Hunger Games*. We often call her Little Rue. *Rue* is also the French word for "street." For this story, I decided to change the spelling of her name to Roo, as in *Winnie-the-Pooh*. Bertie thinks a dog named Little Roo is a bit silly, so he calls her LR for short.

Did agents really use codes?

Yes, but the codes used by actual SOE agents were much more complex than the ones that appear here. Some used key words from original poems. The real Leo Marks, who was in charge of the coding department, sometimes wrote poems for agents.

Are any of the characters based on or inspired by real people?

Yes. Although Bertie, Eleanor, and David are entirely fictional, other characters—such as Warden Ita, Harry Butcher, Leo Marks, and General Eisenhower (and, of course, his Scottish terrier Telek)—are inspired by actual historical figures. You can find the names of the real people who appear in the story in the roster that follows. But in all cases, their actions and dialogue have been fictionalized. (Although I must add that the real Telek did indeed have a reputation for being very hard to housebreak!)

ROSTER OF TERMS, EVENTS
& HISTORICAL FIGURES

Harry Butcher—Harry Butcher was the chief aide to General
    Eisenhower. He wrote a book about his experiences that
    included several anecdotes about Telek.

D-Day—*D-Day* is a military planning term that stands simply
    for the day a battle is to begin (similarly, *H-Hour* is used
    to designate the hour an operation will begin). The most
    famous D-Day in history—and what most people mean when
    they refer to D-Day—took place on June 6, 1944, when
    156,000 Allied troops landed by parachute and by boat on
    five beaches on the coast of Normandy, France.

Dwight D. "Ike" Eisenhower—General Eisenhower arrived in
    London in January of 1944 to lead Operation Overlord as
    the supreme commander of the Allied Expeditionary Force.
    After World War II, Eisenhower would go on to become the
    thirty-fourth president of the United States.

E. Ita Ekpenyon—Ita in the story was inspired by a real person.
    Born in Nigeria, E. Ita Ekpenyon moved to London,
    volunteered as an air-raid warden, and wrote a short memoir
    about his WWII experiences.

Leo Marks—Leo Marks, the son of an antiquarian bookseller,
    became fascinated with codes after reading Edgar Allan Poe's
    story "The Gold-Bug." Marks became the head of coding
    and code deciphering at the SOE. His father's bookstore,

Marks & Co, became famous in a book and film entitled *84 Charing Cross Road*.

Office of Strategic Services (OSS)—The OSS, an American organization, was the forerunner of today's Central Intelligence Agency (CIA). Several college professors from the United States were posted to London to work for the OSS and lived near Grosvenor Square.

Operation Overlord—This was the code name for the Allied plan to invade Europe and ultimately defeat Germany to win the war.

Special Operations Executive (SOE)—With its headquarters on Baker Street, this British organization recruited secret agents to send to countries under German occupation to form and lead sabotage and resistance efforts.